WHAT
Naj

Naji - and the mystery dig by Vahid Imani provides a wonderful window into the Iranian world as seen through the eyes of a young girl. Learn about a Middle Eastern culture, history, religion, geography and cuisine. You will find how basic attributes of laughter, worry, fear, respect, love, kindness, and other human characteristics, are universal, no matter where we live. You will fall in love with Naji as she fascinates you.

-- Dr. Marvin Marshall
Author of *Parenting Without Stress:*
How to Raise Responsible Kids While
Keeping a Life of Your Own

"Naji" is a charming story that would be a very welcome addition to any classroom library. It could be used to enhance both a language arts curriculum and/or a social studies curriculum. I think students will find it interesting and entertaining. I highly recommend it to any parent or educator.

--Bob Neider
Retired educator with 31 years of experience in elementary schools

A charming read that brings to life the sights, sounds, smells, beliefs, and humor of family life in 1942 Iran. An excellent book for parents and educators who wish to explore the culture of this country with their students. I highly recommend it!

--Ellen Beckerman
Elementary school educator

Naji and the mystery of the dig is a delightful, culturally rich story of adventure and intrigue that will be subtly instructive to Naji's age group all around the world, yet bubbling over with the romp and tumble, play and pleasure typical of children in every culture. This is a book that should be on students' summer reading lists. Better yet, it would be ideal as a literary unit, delightfully tasted and experienced together by teachers and students in classrooms in every culture. The author writes so vividly and life-like, the reader will find herself or himself in the story, hearing, smelling, and enjoying Naji's experiences firsthand— almost. If students everywhere learned of the cultures of other children through literature such as "Naji," our younger generations would build bridges of commonality that would become bridges of peace in our world.

--David Gardner
pastor, missionary, world traveler
and retired K-12 principal

A little girl, Naji, takes us inside the family life and cultural values of Iranian society as she grapples with a powerful mystery. Providing cultural understanding of a faraway world in an entertaining and accessible way, this book is highly recommended for children of all ages.

--Dr. Paul H. Gelles

educator, anthropologist, and author of *Andean Lives: Gregorio Condori Mamani and Asunta Quispe Huaman*

Naji

and the
mystery of the dig

Vahid Imani

Stormtop Publishing

P.O. Box 132

Solvang, Ca 93464 U.S.A

www.stormtopublishing.com

Illustrations and cover by Karri Simmon
www.nicedesignonline.com

Editing and proofreading services provided by Jeanette Morris of First Impressions Writing Services,
www.firstimpressionswriting.com

ISBN 978-0-9911103-1-5

ISBN 978-0-9911103-0-8 (hc)

Library of Congress Control Number: 2013953974

Library Subject headings:

1- Mystery-Juvenile fiction. 2- Conduct of life-Juvenile fiction.

3- Cultural Heritage-Fiction. 4- Children's stories-Persian.

5- Folklore-Iran-Juvenile literature. 6- Iran-Juvenile fiction.

7- Iran-Social life and customs-Fiction. 8- Iranians-Fiction.

Lexile® Measures 690L

www.najistories.com

In memory of my mother

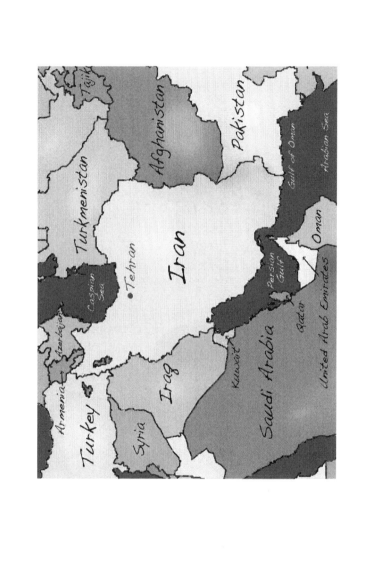

Naji

and the mystery of the dig

Vahid Imani

Stormtop Publishing

Chapter 1

Naji woke up, much too early for her liking, to an unusual sound coming from her courtyard. She rolled over and pulled the blanket over her head, trying to ignore the sound. After all, it was summer in Iran's capital city, Tehran. The season for sleeping late.

Thump … thump … thump. The noise continued. The blanket didn't muffle the sound.

"What *is* that?" she mumbled. The sound seemed familiar to Naji, but never before in *her* yard. The noise went on and on—short and repeating thumps. Deep, but not too deep.

Men's voices joined the thumping. Naji didn't recognize these voices.

"I guess it's time to investigate," she said, even though the rest of her family had long ago left their common sleeping room, and no one could hear her words.

Naji rubbed her large, almond-shaped eyes and rolled off her mat onto the floor. She enjoyed this fun and easy way to get up. She stood and tiptoed to the window, hoping that nobody would see her. She pulled aside the curtain, just enough to peek into the courtyard.

Three strangers holding shovels and pickaxes stood around a hole. One was talking to her father, and the other two were digging the ground at a steady pace. The *thump* ... *thump* sound was the pickaxe hitting the ground.

How odd.

Hearing footsteps outside the room, Naji quickly let the curtain go and jumped back onto her bed. She felt safer there. If the steps were those of a stranger, she could hide under the blanket. If they were Mother's, she might not nag her if she believed Naji was still asleep. The door opened, and Naji peeked out from under the corner of her blanket.

"Oh, it's only you," she muttered.

"Only me?" replied Leila, Naji's older sister, who was eleven. "What do you mean? Anyway, get up lazy girl, there is a lot going on today." Leila opened the cupboard door and began searching through the scarves hanging on hooks.

Naji sat up, but didn't leave her cozy bed. "What's going on outside? Who are those strangers? What are they doing?"

"Father has hired some workers to dig a hole."

"Dig a hole? What for? How deep?"

Leila sighed. "A septic hole. A deep septic hole for a new outhouse."

"A *deep* hole! We have never disturbed the earth by this house before," said Naji.

Leila turned around and faced Naji. "What are you talking about—disturbing the earth?"

"What if they go too far down and agitate the underworld? Are we ready for what might happen?" Naji got up and moved toward the window again.

"*Agitate the underworld*? There's nothing under there but dirt and more dirt," Leila scolded.

Naji felt a knot of panic forming in her stomach. "No, no," she shouted, "they may upset the demons, *looloos,* and *genies.* That's not good. We'll all suffer!"

Leila shook her head and smiled. "Don't worry, little Naji, our father is out there watching. They know what they are doing." Leila began to wind her long, flowing *chador* around herself.

Naji didn't like the way her sister dismissed her worries, but she could see that there was no point in continuing the topic of disturbing the monsters, the *looloos.*

"Do you have to wear your *chador*?" Naji asked.

"Yes, of course. There are strange men here today."

"I thought that inside our house it's okay not to cover ourselves with *chador*."

"You don't have to because you are only eight. I have had to wear it since I was nine," said Leila. "You know very well, Naji, that Islam teaches that no man outside the immediate family is supposed to see a woman's body. So, I wear it to obey God. And, well, I don't want to upset Father."

"You are not a woman! A woman is much older," said Naji, still watching the digging operation from behind the curtain, dressed in her pajama pants and a long tunic that went to her knees.

"But I have started puberty already. I am considered a woman. I must cover myself now from head to toe," Leila said.

"Well, I'm not going to," Naji declared. "It's too hot." She raked her fingers through her shoulder-length brown hair and looked at her older sister's long black waves with envy. "Why are they digging a new septic hole?"

"The other one is full."

"So, I can't use the outhouse now?" Naji asked. "I need to go."

"You can, but not for long."

"Do you know exactly how deep?" Naji crossed her legs. She really needed to go.

"What?"

"How deep are they digging the hole?" Naji asked, louder this time.

"You don't have to shout, Naji. How would I know? I'm sure it is going to be pretty deep. You can ask Father that question yourself." Leila checked her *chador* in the mirror and left the room.

Naji groaned. The knot of panic in her stomach twisted again. "Strangers are bad news," she said to the now-closed door.

Chapter 2

Still dressed in her pajamas, Naji tiptoed to the edge of the short hallway outside the family's main room, with her hand anchored on the wall for balance. Only three steps down to the courtyard. As she approached her grandmother's room across the hallway, she saw the door was closed. Once she got to the edge of the stairs, she peeked around the corner and saw the men.

One worker took the pickaxe up above his head and with all his power hit the ground. The axe's pointed head slammed into the dirt. The other two men used shovels to move the dirt away from the new, growing hole.

Naji cautiously stepped down into the courtyard. Father was smoking a cigarette and talking to one of the men. Across the yard, Mother washed dishes by the utility pool, the *hoze*. It was 1942, and no one in Iran had running water inside the house.

"Good morning, Mother," Naji said as she jumped over the gutter connecting the pool to the city's system of ditches that brought fresh snowmelt from the Alborz Mountains.

"What's so good about it?" her mother grumbled.

The pool water was not fresh, as it should be in the morning. "How come the *hoze* water is so murky, Mother? We should have had some clear water last night. Should I open the latch to get more water?"

"No, we have enough water. Besides, the diggers are making a mess everywhere."

"Can I still use the outhouse?" Naji asked.

"Yes, it can be used for a little while longer." Mother didn't look up at Naji, but continued to wash the dishes.

Mother's bad mood must be from all the commotion and having to wear a *chador* in the yard. She had twisted the white cloth decorated with dark green shamrock prints expertly around her waist. It covered her hair and upper body in such a way that she could squat by the pool and wash the dishes without worrying about it falling off into the water, or slipping off and exposing her hair and body to the workers.

Digging. The word bounced around in Naji's mind. People dig earth to plant a new tree or put a pole in the ground. Gravediggers make holes in the cemetery. But, how does someone dig for a new outhouse? How dark is it down there? Maybe Mother would have answers.

"How deep are they digging?"

Mother glanced up and sighed. "Very deep. Deep enough to last us another thirty years. Long after you are married with children who ask too many questions. Now move on. You have work to do."

Mother's agitated voice confirmed that she was stressed. Naji knew not to press her any more. She hurried toward the outhouse, but kept her eyes on the workers.

The outhouse stood in the corner of the yard at the bottom of a short stairwell. Just as she started down the stairs, Naji looked up to the nearby rooftop to see if the neighbor kids were peeping into her courtyard, as they often did.

Yes, there on the neighbor's roof a shaved head, two large ears, and a pair of eyes spied on her. Naji turned and charged toward the neighbor's house, waving her arms wildly. "Go away, Reza," she shouted. "Go play with your friends in the alley."

She couldn't see any kids playing in the alley, as her courtyard was well protected by their two rooms and a hallway in front and large walls on the sides. But she could hear screaming and knew the sound of these voices well. Reza, the nine-year-old son of the neighbor, disappeared from his rooftop.

"Naji!"

"Yes, Mother, right away," Naji replied, and rushed down the eight steps leading into the outhouse.

A damp, stench-filled darkness surrounded Naji as she reached the bottom of the stairs. There, a small, round hole about the size of her hand opened directly into the sewage chamber. The strong stink was a clear signal that the deep chamber was full, and the need for a new outhouse urgent.

Before Naji squatted over the hole, she held her breath and peered into the darkness of the hole. "I wonder how deep this chamber was when it was first dug?" she said aloud. She recalled her father saying the first outhouse was made over thirty years ago. So, it must be very, very deep to have lasted so long.

"Naji! Hurry up, *Yal-lah*!" Mother started shouting as soon as she saw Naji coming out of the outhouse. "Have your breakfast and get to work."

"But after my breakfast, can I watch the digging?" Naji asked, again staring at the workers and not looking where she was going.

"What is there to look at? They are digging a hole in the ground," said her mother, still washing dishes. Still looking down.

"Please, Mother, I have never seen diggers dig in the yard before."

"Only for a few minutes, then, and only after you wash your breakfast dishes and put them away."

"Thank you, Mother," Naji replied, flashing her best smile. Of course, Mother didn't see it, as her eyes stayed focused on her work in the utility pool.

Naji glanced again at the workers. Already, a pile of freshly dug dirt was forming. Strange thoughts began to swirl in her mind, and then, a quick, unexpected shiver tingled up her spine. Naji took a deep breath, shook her head to clear it, and rushed back toward the main room to eat her breakfast. Too bad this digging didn't start next week. By then the wooden platforms for their summer beds would be up from the basement, and she could sit in the courtyard, eat her breakfast, and watch the digging at the same time.

The summer beds looked like a big deck outside the large windows leading to the sunken courtyard. Once the windows were open, the beds provided a pleasant extension of the family room to the yard. Large peach trees in the courtyard made the area shady. Jasmine vines flowered on the wall next to the bed, scenting the air with their perfume. At night, a large net was placed around the beds to protect the family against hungry mosquitoes. Naji loved a good night's sleep out in the cool summer air.

"Naji, did you finish your breakfast yet?" Her sister interrupted her thoughts by yelling at her from the other side of the yard.

"No, but I'm on it. I will finish it soon," Naji answered. Now Leila, as well as Mother, was nervous about all the work they would have to do to accommodate the unusual presence of workers and her father.

A rustling in the doorway startled Naji. She sucked in a quick breath and turned around to see her tiny, white-haired grandmother emerging from her room. Naji let out her breath and giggled. "Good morning!"

"What is all this racket? Who are these men? What are they doing?" Grandmother asked, but didn't wait for a reply. Holding her bad knee with her left hand, she stepped gingerly into the yard and went straight toward her daughter, Naji's mother, for some answers.

This was getting interesting. Why couldn't the summer beds be out already? Naji took her slippers off and entered the family room. In the corner of the room, a *samovar* was keeping the teapot warm. Many Iranian families carried on the tradition from old Persia to use a *samovar* to boil water to make hot tea. With this system, tea was always ready for guests or anyone who wanted it during the day. Grandmother had told Naji that their *samovar* came from Russia.

Something was not right about this digging. Naji poured her tea, took a piece of fresh *sangãk* bread and some feta cheese. The *sangãk* was her favorite. Usually, though, they only had *lavash* bread. Maybe Mother was serving the better bread because of the workers. Naji took the teapot, which was placed on top of the *samovar* to keep warm, and poured more tea into a small clear glass. The clarity of the amber-colored liquid made her smile. She poured a small spoonful of sugar into her tea and examined it very closely before she stirred it.

"What are you doing? Wasting time, trying to get out of doing your chores?" Leila scolded as she entered the room.

"No, I'm trying to make two-colored tea, but it's not working," Naji answered.

"You don't get two colors like that. First, you need clear hot water. Then you add sugar to the hot water, stir it well, and then you add the hot tea very carefully. More importantly, you need to start helping me before Mother gets even more upset."

"Will the amber go to the bottom or stay on top?" Naji asked, ignoring her sister's warning.

"The clear water stays at the bottom and amber color tea on top. Now, can you please finish eating your breakfast and start helping me out?"

"Just the way I want it, not too hot and not too cold," Naji said about the tea after she added some hot water from the faucet of the *samovar's* boiler. It wasn't that she wanted to be rude to her sister or to antagonize her, she was just interested in experiencing new things. For Naji, life was full of amazement.

Naji finished her breakfast quickly. Then, after turning the small knob at the bottom of the *samovar* to lower the heat a little, but still keep the water warm inside the boiler, she took the dishes down to the pool to wash. Her mother was not there. Naji couldn't take her eyes off the workers and the digging. It was like a strong, strange force pulled her toward it.

Naji squatted by the pool, her eyes on her father and the diggers instead of what was in her hands. As she was setting down her breakfast dishes, a saucer slipped from her hand and sank to the bottom of the pool.

"What are you doing there?" Mother's thunderous voice bellowed just as Naji watched the saucer's gradual disappearance into the murky green water.

"I am washing my breakfast dishes. What would you like me to do first Mother?" She asked politely in her sweetest voice while rinsing off the rest of the dishes.

"There is a stack of lima beans in the room. Start cleaning them," Mother commanded.

"Are they for lunch?" asked Naji.

"Yes, so hurry up, time is running out."

"Can I put a mat outside in the yard and clean the lima beans there?" Naji hoped for a "yes" from her mother. She wanted to watch the workers.

"No," her mother responded firmly.

Naji went for a second try. "What if Leila and I do it together in the yard?"

"I said, no. I don't want these men to get distracted by you two." This time she was firm and agitated.

"Yes, Mother, right away," Naji replied quickly. She knew what could come next if she kept begging, and it wasn't pretty. Her mother's temper was not something to toy with.

Naji went back to the main room but could not avoid watching the workers on her way, stumbling once or twice as she walked. Inside the room, her sister had already started working on a pile of lima beans.

"Can you work on the dill and leave the lima beans for me?" Naji asked. Lima beans were not the only ingredients of the dish her mother would prepare for lunch. But the lima beans were the most fun for Naji. She liked squeezing them open and popping the seeds out of the pods.

"First, you need to finish washing your breakfast dishes, and then negotiate. Didn't you see how agitated Mother was?"

"I did that already." Naji plopped down on the floor next to her sister and started working on the lima beans. Leila had spread a sheet on the floor on top of the carpet to keep it clean. She was sitting on the sheet next to the stack of lima beans and other greens.

"Where is our brother today?" Naji asked.

"Ali got a part time job at Hassan Agha's grocery store."

"Does he know that we are digging the yard?"

"Yes, he does."

"I'm sure he can't wait 'til he gets home to watch."

"What is your fascination with these ditch diggers?" Leila asked.

"Don't you find it mysterious?"

"Mysterious? No, I find it dirty, messy, and smelly, and it brings a bunch of strangers into our house. I hate it. Especially because I have to cover myself with this stupid *chador* in my own house."

"But what if they find a nest of snakes? Or what if they find a treasure?" Naji, oblivious to her sister's frustration and lack of imagination, continued to fantasize about the excavation.

"There are snakes everywhere. I am not afraid of them, or anything else, for that matter. And there are no treasures in our yard. Naji, don't play with the beans, just finish the job. Mother will need these soon."

Naji, unimpressed by her sister's demand, continued to enjoy shooting the lima bean seeds out of their shells. "Look, it's fun. Don't you want to do this? We can see who can shoot the seed the farthest." Naji squished another shell and shot the bean across the carpet.

"No, and I don't want Mother to pull my ear. She will be very upset if the greens are not cleaned soon."

Leila's reply brought Naji back to reality. The two sisters cleaned the greens and shelled the lima beans, then took them back to their mother. She was in the kitchen across the yard.

"Mother, it is time for the workers to have some hot tea. May I take it to them?" Naji hoped her ploy would get her closer to the digging site. By getting closer to the dig, she might discover the reason for her strong attraction to it.

"Yes, yes, go ahead, but be careful not to break anything, and make sure you pour your father's tea in his favorite big glass," Mother said. She raised her voice toward the end of her instructions, because Naji started running back to the room the moment she heard the first yes.

Naji grabbed the flat silver platter and placed a set of four tea glasses and saucers on it. She made sure one of them was her father's favorite. She added a

sugar cube dish and one teaspoon for each person. She poured tea in all four glasses, placed the teapot on the platter, and got up. But the teapot made the platter too heavy for her to carry.

She put the platter down carefully and placed the teapot back on top of the *samovar*.

"I will come back for you if they ask for more tea." She spoke to the teapot. "I don't want to create any trouble that would keep me from getting closer to the digging." Then Naji carefully lifted the platter again.

On her way, she watched the tray closely to avoid any spillage. She admired the asymmetric shapes of the sugar cubes. Each one had its own unique shape; no two were alike. Her mother, just recently, had used a special hammer to break the large cones of sugar into smaller pieces. She hoped that one day Mother would allow her to break up the cones.

"Hello, *Salahm*," Naji said to her father, bringing the tray of tea.

"*Salahm*, my dear daughter. So, you are up and bringing us some tea." Father's voice was cheery—even jubilant.

"Oh Father, I have been up for a while! I have already had breakfast and cleaned the lima beans for lunch."

"Oh, you have? Good girl."

Naji held the tray while Father picked up his glass of hot tea, a saucer, a few sugar cubes, and a teaspoon. The workers saw Naji and her tray, put their tools down, and came to have their hot tea. She did not know the pecking order, so she offered tea to the closest worker.

"The foreman first, please," said the worker pointing to his supervisor who was standing behind him. The worker did not touch the tea, but used a two-handed gesture to offer it to his foreman, a short, chubby man with a thick, black beard. Naji understood the custom of higher-ranking people eating first. She stepped toward the foreman and offered him tea. Then she offered it to the other workers. Each of the workers picked up a glass of hot tea, a saucer, and a few sugar cubes, but none of them picked up a teaspoon.

Naji's nostrils flared at the smell of damp, freshly dug dirt from the pile near the opening of the hole. She placed the tray on the ground and walked toward the pile. She peeked at the pile. In her most respectful tone she asked, "Father, what are you doing?"

"Well, we are digging a new septic hole," Father explained.

She examined the dirt pile, dark brown and almost velvety. She went near the hole, extended her neck, and tried to see down into it.

"Be careful, Naji! Don't get too close to the edge. You may fall and hurt yourself," Father warned.

"Did you find many snake nests?" Naji asked.

"Snake nests?" The foreman's eyes crinkled as he smiled broadly. Then the other men laughed as they poured their hot tea into the saucers.

"No, dear, we have not discovered any snake nests yet," her father said, and then rolled the sugar cube in his mouth to sweeten the bitter tea.

"How about dead people, have you found any dead bodies yet?"

Naji's serious question was followed by one of the workers muffling his burst of laughter by blowing into his saucer to cool his tea. Then by another roar of laughter from everyone.

"Why are you laughing? Dead people are not funny. You should be careful. While you are digging, when you least expect it, a hand may come from under the dirt and pull you underground," Naji continued, surprised that they didn't know of the unpleasant and unexpected dangers of messing with the underworld.

"My dear daughter, your imagination is working overtime. Don't worry, these men are professionals, and they know what they are doing." Father turned and joined the workers in their continuing laughter.

"Yes, and we have our weapons with us to defend ourselves," said one of the men, chuckling as he lifted his shovel.

More laughter from the men.

"My dear Naji, go and bring us the teapot. We need more tea," Father requested.

Naji stomped back toward the house, mumbling to herself as she went. "Consider yourselves warned."

Chapter 3

Naji grabbed the teapot from the *samovar* and brought it back to her father. The men were still laughing. He took the teapot and poured more tea for all the men and then some for himself.

Stepping carefully toward the pile of dirt to examine it further, Naji noticed worms wiggling around, trying to save themselves from diving sparrows and curious crows. Naji moved even closer to the hole and peeked inside. The cool air from the deep dark gently touched her face. She felt a chilling sensation, some sort of eerie tranquility, as if, deep underneath, something was patiently waiting for the right time.

Frightened, she dashed back to the main room, forgetting the teapot, not knowing exactly what she was running from. She was just scared, and wanted to hide under her blanket

But her bed was no longer there. Someone had put it away in the back end of the room, where an indentation similar to a closet without a door stored the bedding during the daytime. All the bedding was hidden behind a curtain. Naji jumped behind the curtain and grabbed the nearest bedding, hugging it to her face. Its soft and familiar smell comforted her. She just wasn't sure why.

"Naji? Naji, where are you?" Leila yelled as she rushed into the room about twenty minutes later. "Father is looking for you!"

"Here," Naji responded from behind the curtain.

"Where are you, I can't see you. Are you hiding?"

"No. I'm not hiding from you." It wasn't a lie. She wasn't hiding from her sister.

Leila moved the curtain to find Naji playing with some dolls in the little space between the curtain and the mountain of folded bedding.

"So, here you are. What are you hiding from?"

"I am not hiding. I am playing," Naji retorted, trying to hide the real reason she was in there.

"Well, play time is over. Mother asked me to find you and have you help me sweep the carpet in here."

"Oh, come and sit down with me. Let's play with my dolls a little bit." Naji tapped the floor next to her a couple of times. Using her powers of persuasion, she continued. "Lady Nargess wants you to play with her." She held one of her dolls up to her sister's face.

Leila smiled. "Okay, but just for a little bit. And then, will you help me sweep this room?"

"Yes," Naji answered with a smile and enthusiasm.

After a few minutes of playing, Naji had a clever idea. Holding the Nargess doll up toward her sister's doll, she asked in her best, pretend high voice, "Do you think Hell is under ground?"

"I don't know. Some say it is up in the heavens and some say it's underground," Leila answered in the pretend voice of her doll, Lady Zohreh.

Naji smiled to herself. Her sister had played along as she had hoped. "Here, Lady Zohreh, have some cookies. I will have some myself, too. Yahmm, aren't they delicious?" Naji continued the game, extending the arm of her doll to offer a pretend cookie to her sister's doll.

"Yahmm, they're quite delicious. Did you make them yourself?" Leila's doll asked.

"No, I don't know how to make cookies."

"Then who gave them to you?"

"The monsters underground gave them to me."

"What are you saying? Are you crazy?" Leila put the doll down. "That's it!

I am not playing anymore." Her voice returned to her normal, scolding one. "Come on. We've got to do our chore."

"Okay," Naji said calmly. But in truth, she was disappointed that her plan failed.

Since the room was used often, cleaning the carpet was a daily chore that Naji knew how to do, but did not enjoy.

"Where is my *jaroo*?"

"Here." Leila handed Naji the triangular broom made from the leaves of the *jaroo* bush. The carpet had a lot of dust, and Leila had to cover her mouth and nose with her scarf during the sweeping.

"Never mind. Help me with the dust pan," said Leila, noticing that Naji was still too short for the sweeping part.

"Do you think they will find *looloo* monsters or *Ahl* demons down there?" asked Naji.

"What did you say?" Leila asked. The sound of the broom brushing against the carpet made it difficult for her to hear.

"Do you think they will find *looloos* down there?"

"Where?"

"Down there in the hole, deep underground, where the men are digging."

Leila stopped sweeping, straightened up her back, and glared at Naji. "Are you serious?" Leila asked with a note of surprise in her voice.

"Every time I go near the pool, people say, 'Be careful , don't get too close to the edge or the pool's *looloo* will come up and grab you and take you down underneath the water.' When I go to the door to look out into the alley, someone says, 'Be careful, don't go too far or the alley *looloo* will take you.' Anywhere that is dangerous, someone says there is a *looloo* monster that will take the children. So I figure there must be demons such as *looloo* and *Ahl* down in the septic hole too."

Leila frowned, making her luscious, dark eyebrows nearly touch. Naji expected her to have a ready answer, as she always did. But Leila surprised her by remaining silent and looking away for a moment.

"You don't have anything to be afraid of, little Naji," Leila finally said, concentrating on the sweeping once again. "Stop making excuses for not doing chores with me. There are no *looloo* monsters underneath the ground. And where did you hear about *Ahl*?"

"I overheard our mother telling a pregnant woman that she needed to do something that I didn't understand, otherwise, *Ahl* demon would come and grab or eat her baby," Naji answered.

"Oh, that is entirely different. There are no monsters or anything else underneath the ground," Leila reassured her sister.

"But I think there is *something* down there. I can feel it," Naji confessed.

"Don't be silly, Naji. Pay attention to your work. That will take your mind off this monster business."

"I am serious, Leila. I can smell it. I will show you. Let's go, but you need to be brave." Naji was not going to drop the issue. Not this time.

Chapter 4

"Okay, Naji. I will play along with your game. You have made me a little curious about the hole. But, let's finish this job first," Leila finally agreed.

Once the sisters finished sweeping and tidying the room, they went out into the yard and cautiously approached the new dig.

"I wonder if genies will creep out of the hole," Leila teased. "You know, Naji, that genies are mentioned in the *Qur'an*."

"Do you really believe in genies, sister?" Naji asked as they approached the dig. "I thought you didn't believe in anything supernatural anymore."

Leila laughed and tousled Naji's hair. "So, here we are. I can't smell anything in the air except sautéed onions coming from the kitchen. And my stomach is rumbling now with the promise of Mother's delicious lunch."

"Don't get too close to the edge, girls," said Father, watching his daughters' every move.

"But Father, can't we please look into the hole?" asked Naji with the most polite and innocent voice she could muster.

"Okay, but let me hold your hands. We shouldn't get in the way of the men working." Father reached out his hands, and holding them both tightly, brought them close to the edge of the hole.

"This freshly dug earth does smell different, Naji," Leila said. "But I can't see anything mysterious here. Just a man down in the hole, filling a bucket with more dirt so the other two men can pull the bucket up, empty it, and send it down again."

"Father?" asked Naji.

"Yes," Father replied.

"Ah, is—"

"How much deeper are they going to dig?" Leila interrupted.

"Oh, much deeper. They should go about fifteen meters," Father answered.

"How deep is it now?"

Leila's matter-of-fact questioning was getting on Naji's nerves. Her sister was wasting precious time with Father and distracting him from Naji's more important questions. She decided to be much firmer and not allow Leila to cut her off again.

"About two meters, maybe three," Father answered.

"Won't it get dark for the diggers?" Naji asked.

"Yes, the deeper he digs the darker it will become. But you don't need to worry about him. He will use a lantern when it gets too dark."

"Isn't he afraid of *looloo*?" Naji persisted, with concern in her voice.

"*Looloo*?" her father repeated, then pressed his lips together so he wouldn't laugh. He smiled and glanced at the other workers.

They were chuckling again.

"Yes, *looloo*. Mother says *looloo* monsters are everywhere," Naji replied firmly. She scowled at the men for taking the matter lightly.

Her father tried to control his laughter by pressing his lips more tightly together. Then he nodded. "Yes, your mother is right, but *looloos* only take little kids, they are afraid of adults."

Naji was puzzled by her father's answer, but not ready to give up her probing. She was about to ask something else when she heard a sound coming from the street.

"Oh, Leila! Do you hear that?" Naji shouted, her eyes wide open.

"Yes!" Leila shouted back, suddenly behaving like a little girl again.

The two sisters looked at each other and ran toward the street door.

"Wait!" Father's thunderous voice pinned them to the spot.

Chapter 5

"It's the ice cream man!"

It was the first time that Naji had heard the shout of the ice cream man since the start of summer. The call was accompanied by the ring of a bell, which was the happiest sound Naji had heard that day. She had to put the mystery of the hole aside, for now.

Although her body wanted to rush to the door, her mind stopped to obey her father's command. Naji's heart pounded so hard, she could feel the vibrations throughout her body. Leila stood waiting just a few meters ahead of her.

"I will get you the ice cream. Leila, put on your *chador*," ordered Father.

"Yes, Father, it fell when I ran," Leila replied while quickly putting the *chador* back over her head.

Their father was rarely home during weekdays. Naji relished this rare opportunity to do something delightful with him. But he was also the protector of his family's virtue, *nahmoos*. He had to make sure Leila was covered before she went out on the street where there could be many strange men. Naji smiled inside that she was still too young to be required to wear a *chador*.

Their street door wasn't a big door, but it was made of thick, heavy wood. "I will open the door," Leila said.

Naji couldn't wait. She jumped out as the door was half opened. "Ahh!" she screamed, and fell back into Leila.

"Watch out!" a bicyclist shouted as he was speeding away.

"Oh, that was close," said Naji, her palm pressed against her pumping heart.

Their street door opened up to a wide, busy alley that connected two wider streets together. People, bicyclists, street vendors, cats, and birds were typical travelers in their alley.

"Be careful, Naji! You need to always peek before jumping out," scolded Leila.

"You are right, of course. Oh, there he is!" Naji pointed at the ice cream man and ran toward him.

"Wait for Father," Leila yelled.

During the day, many vendors walked up and down the streets and alleys, shouting or singing out the names of the crafts, food, or services they sold. Their songs were often rhyming and melodious. Many vendors packed their donkeys or hand carts with fruits and vegetables and called out "selling greens, tomatoes, and cucumbers."

Naji's favorite street vendors in the summertime were the ice cream man and the *faloodeh* man. *Faloodeh* was a delicious frozen dessert made of thin vermicelli noodles, cornstarch, rose water, lime juice, crushed ice, and sometimes ground pistachios.

The daily chorus of vendors combined with the noises of bicycle horns, motorcycle engines, and donkey calls created the typical background sound in Naji's crowded neighborhood. Today, Naji focused so much on the ice cream vendor that she missed the call of the vegetable vendor and almost ran into him in her rush for the ice cream.

"Wait for Father!" Leila yelled again to no avail. Naji was already jumping up and down by the ice cream vendor's handcart.

"Look, Leila, he's the same man who sells cooked beets in the winters," Naji exclaimed.

"Yes, that's correct little lady. I sell cooked beets too. What a fine memory," said the ice cream vendor.

Naji's mouth watered as she watched the vendor take a round wafer in his hand, then scoop the ice cream, slap it on the wafer, and put another round wafer on top, making an ice cream sandwich.

She loved the special stretchy ice cream flavored with rose water and saffron.

"Here Naji, don't spill it," Father said as he handed her the long sought-after treat. "And here is yours, Leila."

"Thank you, Father. But I wish the sour green plums and green almonds would come soon. Those are my favorite summer treats."

"Oh, yes! Green almonds with a sprinkle of salt. Yum! I can't wait to hear that vendor's call," said Naji.

"In two weeks, you will," said the ice cream man.

"Leila, let's count to see whose ice cream has more pistachios," Naji challenged her sister. The two girls engaged in an energetic pursuit of counting, and more importantly, licking while turning their ice cream sandwich. What was happening in the outside world didn't matter anymore. Even the hole and diggers were all forgotten during those glorious ice cream moments.

From the nearby street, the melodious call of a pool man announced his service of emptying and cleaning the pools. But Naji blocked out the sounds and business of the street and focused all her attention on eating her delicious ice cream sandwich, challenging herself not to waste a single drop. Until ...

"*Na-ma-kie*! *Noon-e-khoshck*! Salt blocks! Dried breads."

Naji froze, distracted from her ice cream frenzy. She looked at the direction of the sound and found the source of the call. She gasped, then bit her bottom lip,

horrified. A bear of a man in ragged clothing lumbered toward her pulling a skinny white donkey.

"*Na-ma-kie*! *Noon-e khoshck*! Salt blocks! Dried breads!" he shouted, his voice loud and resonating. Naji's heart pounded so loudly she could hear it.

As the man came closer, Naji could make out his rough face and beard. The poor old donkey had such a large load that she was sure it would collapse any moment. The dirt and mud caked on the donkey's feet showed a long, difficult journey for the pair. The scary man yanked and pulled on the donkey's rope, still shouting, *"Na-ma-kie, noon-e-khoshck."*

Naji moved close to her father and tried to hide behind his legs. It was when she actually clutched her father's legs in fear that he noticed Naji's unease.

"What is it, Naji? Why are you trembling?"

Naji tried to answer him, but could not make words come out of her mouth.

The best she could do was point to the gruff man with the dirty white donkey.

Chapter 6

"Are you pointing to the *namakie*? You know what that means. He buys dried bread and pays for it with rock salt blocks. You know—the white rocks that your mother grinds to season our food. She buys them from him." Father's words made sense, but Naji held his legs tighter and continued to hide.

"Maybe because of his accent you don't understand him. He is saying *na-ma-kie*, salt block, and *noon-e-khoshck*, dried bread," her father repeated in a clear accent. But that was not Naji's problem. She understood the big man quite well.

As he got closer, Naji noticed that the *namakie* was missing some front teeth and his saliva was leaking on his beard when he shouted. She was so scared that she didn't notice her forgotten ice cream, melting into a puddle of drips on the ground.

"Naji, watch out! Your ice cream is about to fall," Leila warned.

"He ... he is monster *Looloo Namakie*," Naji said, her quivering voice barely a whisper. She squeezed her father's leg with her free hand and pointed to the man with the donkey using her ice cream sandwich.

"What? Monster *Looloo Namakie*? Ha!"

Naji peered into Father's face, confused by his chuckle. Then his face grew serious.

"You are right, of course, little Naji, to be cautious of all strangers, and especially the street vendors. You should stay near me. Remember, they are harmless when you are near an adult."

Leila had a strange grin on her face. She winked at Father, as if they shared a secret. Naji didn't like being left out of secrets.

"Okay, girls, now that you have had your ice creams, it is time to go back home and see what the diggers are doing."

Naji followed the *namakie's* every move with her watchful eyes, still clinging to her father, as they walked back to their front door. Naji heard another vendor shouting. This time it was a mattress fluffer, *lahaf-dooz*. Her father stopped.

"Leila, go tell your mother that I am hiring a mattress fluffer," Father ordered.

"Also help her bring the mattresses into the yard."

Leila rushed to find her mother.

Naji followed Leila into the house, but ran directly to her grandmother's room as soon as she heard that a *lahaf-dooz* would be in their house. Grandmother sat on the ground with a needle in one hand and black thread in the other. A black sock lay across her knee.

"Grandma, can I hide here for a little while?" Naji asked.

Grandmother arched her eyebrows in alarm, making the nostrils of her wide nose flare out. "Why, little Naji? What is wrong?"

"When I was on the street eating my ice cream, I saw a *Looloo Namakie* and now a *Looloo Lahaf-dooz* is coming into the house," said Naji, gasping for air while describing her encounter with all the monsters she had seen on the street.

Grandmother stared at Naji for a second and blinked her dark eyes a few times. "Oh, good, then, just in time to help me. You have strong eyes, my dear. Pass this thread through the needle's eye. I want to patch the hole in my sock before I go help your mother."

"Can I sew the hole too? I swear I can do it. Mother has taught me how to patch holes," Naji begged.

"All right, but be careful, my dear. I don't want you to hurt yourself."

Naji's small but steady hands, combined with her good eyesight, easily accomplished the task. Like an expert tailor, she sewed the hole with confidence. The task calmed Naji.

"So, Grandma, if the mattress fluffer, *lahaf-dooz* is a *looloo* why does Father bring him into our house?" Naji asked.

"Well, my dear, mattress fluffer, *lahaf-dooz* will become a monster, a *looloo,* if you are alone on the street. But *lahaf-doozes* are the best ones to fluff the cotton and fix mattresses. They are harmless if adults are around," Grandmother explained.

"Is it the same as other *looloos*, such as *Looloo Namakie*, the salt trader?"

"Yes, all *looloos* are harmless when adults are around. Actually, they are rather useful. Now, I better go and help your mother. It seems that she has her hands full today. Help me get up, dear," Grandmother asked. With her old age and bad knees, she always needed help. "Hold my hand."

"Oh, yes, of course," Naji replied. She helped her grandmother get up and held her hands until she was clear of the hallway stairs and safely into the yard.

Grandmother glanced at the dig operation and shook her head. Then she shook her hands free of Naji's grasp and started her wobbly walk toward the kitchen across the courtyard.

Naji hoped Grandma was right. But if *looloos* were not dangerous when adults were around, and they acted and looked like humans, was it possible that they were some form of human?

Naji walked back toward the main room, but she did not intend to go there. She wanted a place to hide—and observe.

Chapter 7

Naji found a shady corner in her yard, far enough from the mattress fluffer to be safe, but close enough to observe him.

He kept his eyes on his work of fluffing the mattresses. She spied on him for over an hour, and he never stopped working. He did not show any monster-like behavior. As a matter of fact, he was very courteous to her mother and father when they spoke to him. Naji had seen a mattress fluffer, *lahaf-dooz,* before—on the streets, in her own house, as well as in the homes of relatives and friends. Never once had a *lahaf-dooz* acted like a monster, *looloo.* Of course, adults had always been present. Still ...

After some heavy thinking and connecting a few stray dots, she had an idea. If it turned out to be true, her life would change dramatically.

It was time to test her idea. Phase one: "observation." She continued watching him.

The mattress fluffer carefully took all the cotton out of the mattresses and piled it up in a small white mountain. Then he put a single-stringed tool like a large bow called *kaman*, into the middle of the mountain. He lifted a large, hammer-shaped mallet and started pounding the *kaman* with hard blows.

Pieces of cotton floated in the air like snowflakes, dancing to *lahaf-dooz's* tune. The vibration of the single string on the *kaman* separated the cotton pieces

from each other and tossed them on the air. The "plunk" coming from the string's vibration and his steady pounding rhythm created a unique music, similar to a one-stringed bass fiddle.

It was time to launch the second phase of the test of her idea: "contact." Deep in thought, she startled when her sister's voice jolted her.

"Didn't you hear Father calling you?"

"No." Naji stood up and brushed off her tunic.

"Hurry up, see what he wants," Leila said.

Naji ran to her father, who was still helping the diggers.

"Yes, Father, did you call me?"

"I did. It is time for another round of hot tea."

"Right away, Father."

She ran to the room, organized several tea glasses on the platter, and started pouring hot tea. As she was pouring, her thoughts drifted to the *lahaf-dooz* and how she could start the "contact" phase.

"Naji! Look what you have done!" her sister shouted. "Tea is spilled everywhere, on the saucers, tray, over the sugar cube holder. What a mess!"

"Oh, sorry, I will clean it," Naji replied with a sheepish smile. The mess didn't matter. She had just figured out how to initiate contact.

"It seems your mind is somewhere else. I will take the tea to Father," Leila scolded.

"No, no. I will do it. I promise I will pay attention," Naji begged. If her sister interfered, her plan would be spoiled.

"All right, but I am watching you!"

Naji cleaned the spills and took the tea to her father. Carefully holding the tray with all the tea items on it, she offered tea to everybody near the dig, one by one.

"Father, should I take tea to the *lahaf-dooz* too? He has been working very hard without a break for a long time now." With that question, she officially started phase two of her quest.

"Yes, go ahead," Father replied.

Naji rushed back to the main room and organized another tea tray. She could barely contain her joy that her plan was working so easily.

Her approach was careful and vigilant. Like a curious cat approaching an unknown adversary, she was alert and ready to run if he tried to attack her.

"Excuse me, excuse me," Naji had to yell so her delicate voice could overcome the loud noise of the *lahaf-dooz's* equipment. He noticed her and stopped pounding.

"*Salahm Agha*, hello mister," she continued in a softer voice. "My father asked me to bring you hot tea."

Little pieces of cotton danced to the ground and settled. The man set his equipment aside and waited for her to put down the tray, not speaking a single word.

Naji waited for all the dust and cotton to settle. Tea does not taste good with pieces of cotton floating in it. Finally, Naji carefully set the tray on the ground near him.

"Thank you, little lady. May God return your kindness to you many times over in heaven," he said, pulling the tray nearer.

Naji stayed frozen in place, studying him carefully. He was an old man with dark, leather-like skin. His fingers were thick and calloused. He wore a white felt cap, big enough to cover his bald spot. Because he sat on the ground, they were at the same eye level.

"How old are you, Miss?" he asked in a thick accent, his eyes fixed on the tea glass. He was not from her city of Tehran. Maybe from a village, by the sound of his words. He glanced her way with his dark, beady eyes. Again, behaving politely, not making eye contact.

"Eight," she replied hesitantly, also not looking him in the eyes, but still staying vigilant.

"I have a granddaughter your age," he said.

"What is her name?"

"Miriam."

"Miriam?"

"Yes."

"Is she a human?"

"What? What did you say?"

"Is Miriam a human?"

"Let's see, are you a human?" he asked, a hint of laughter in his voice.

"Yes! Of course I am," Naji replied.

"She is just like you, so she must be a human too." The *lahaf-dooz* smiled.

Naji opened her mouth to ask something else, but shut it again when Father's voice carried across the courtyard.

"Naji! Come back now!"

Lahaf-dooz had finished his tea, so she took the tray from the ground. But instead of going directly toward Father, she decided to go the other way. The other way would first take her by the digging area. When she got close to the dig site, she glanced at her father to see if he was watching her. Good, he wasn't.

She adjusted her path and went even closer. She could feel cool air coming from the hole. Its presence pulled her toward it, mysteriously. When she got to the edge, she extended her neck and looked inside. "There must be something down there. I can feel it," she whispered.

"Naji!" Her father called. "Where are you? We are finished with our tea. You can take the dishes away."

"Yes, right away," Naji called out, backing away from the hole, but not before another shiver crept up her spine.

After taking the tea dishes back to the main room, Naji went back to her observation post. Mulling over her encounter with *lahaf-dooz*, she felt a bit confused. He didn't act or speak like the monster that Mother warned about. On the contrary, he seemed like a kindly grandfather. His behavior was obedient, courteous, kind, and focused on the work he was hired to do. He spoke, dressed, and acted just like a human. How could he be a monster that steals little children?

It was time for phase three.

Chapter 8

Naji went to the pool, put her knees on the edge, bent over, and brought her face down to the surface of the water. So close, that the water kissed her nose.

"Naji!" her mother screamed from across the yard.

Naji raised her head. "Yes, Mother."

"What are you doing? Get away from the pool."

"I am trying to see the bottom of the pool."

"Why?"

"I am looking for *looloo*," Naji replied honestly.

Naji held her position and looked harder into the deep, green water. Not that she wanted to disobey her mother, but she was so close to solving the mystery. She could see the red fish and the black fish only when they came close to the surface. She kept her gaze on the red fish as they descended, hoping to follow them all the way to the bottom. But she lost them in the darkness of the green water.

Perhaps a white rock would be visible on the bottom. It was worth a try. With all the digging, finding a suitable white rock was not difficult. She found a large flat one, went back to the edge of the pool, and assumed her previous position. She held the white rock in her left hand, very near her face, and then gently let it go. The small ripples created by the rock caused the water to touch her nose again and blurred her vision a bit. She watched

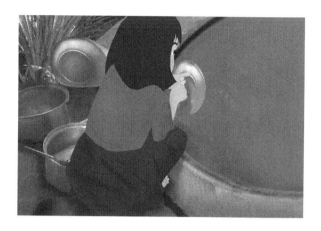

the white rock disappear into the depths of the dark green water. Another failure. Perhaps something shiny would work better.

Naji started a search for a shiny object. Most of her mother's cooking dishes were shiny, silver-colored pots and pans. To get results, she would have to be brave and persistent. Going through with the third phase required daring actions. She knew that if she were caught, she would be punished. But the deed needed to be done if she were to get to the bottom of the mystery and test her idea. With her mind made up, she walked downstairs to the kitchen, where her mother was working hard to prepare lunch for all the extra people.

"Can I wash the pots and pans for you, Mother? she asked.

Before Mother could answer, Father appeared in the doorway. "I need more help with the digging. I am going to Mr. Hassan's grocery store to get Ali out of his work. Do you need anything from the store?"

"Yes, get a kilo of potatoes, and with all these extra people, you may want to stop by a tea house and get one or two pots of lamb stew, *ahb-gusht*. The lunch I am preparing may not be enough," Mother replied.

Naji was not surprised that Mother worried about having enough food, a common worry with the mothers of all her friends. Naji's mouth watered at the news of the lamb stew. "Oh, I love the potatoes and garbanzo beans in lamb stew. May I have a pot too?" Naji asked.

"No," Mother replied firmly. "It's only for the workers."

Naji understood that her mother was overwhelmed. She took advantage of the opportunity and offered her help again.

"Mother, can I wash the pots and pans for you?"

"Yes, that's a good idea." Mother handed her a tub of dishes.

Naji climbed up the steep steps of the kitchen with a satisfied smile on her face. But when she reached the yard, she spotted her sister at the edge of the pool, washing clothes.

Not wanting any witnesses to her deed, Naji moved to a corner of the pool, away from her sister. Leila turned her head when Naji picked a corner away from her, but she didn't say anything. Naji started scrubbing the pots.

Which pot would be the best to drop? The chosen pot had to be one that her mother would not immediately miss. It also needed to be large enough to be visible while on the bottom of the pool. She decided on a medium-sized aluminum pot. She set it aside and started washing the other ones. First, she splattered water from the pool onto the dishes, added some soap powder, and started scrubbing them. After scrubbing came rinsing.

She looked up to see if her sister was still there. Yes, she was still washing clothes. No more time to wait for Leila to disappear.

To rinse, Naji had to dip the pans into the pool three times, because it was the custom. Conveniently, the ill-fated pot slipped from her hands on the second dip.

She watched the pot slowly sink to the bottom of the pool. The reflection of sunlight from the shiny metal helped her to see the bottom of the pool where it lay. A few fish, curious about the new object, swam over it.

Naji and her sister had swum in that pool many times before during hot summer days. But not this year, as the summer had just begun. They always swam in the pool when her mother or grandmother was watching. Last year, the water was up to her chin when she stood on her toes. She watched for a while to see if any sort of hand or creature other than the fish would take the shiny bait. She was so absorbed in her experiment that she forgot the time.

"Naji!" her mother shouted. Again.

"Yes, Mother." Naji pulled back from bending over the pool.

"What are you doing? Are you done with the dishes yet?"

"Yes, Mother," she replied, then collected the clean pans and stood. Her sister raised her head from her work.

"I saw what you did," Leila said.

"Please don't tell Mother," Naji begged in a whisper.

"Why shouldn't I?"

"I will share a secret with you," Naji said, hoping to bribe her sister. "Plus, it's not as if the pan is lost. Soon the pool man will drain and clean the pool. We will get it back then," she reasoned.

"So, what is the secret?" Leila whispered.

"Naji!" Mother yelled again.

"Yes, Mother, right away!"

Naji turned her head toward her sister and put her index finger on the tip of her nose. "Ssss," she whispered. Trusting her sister to keep quiet, Naji rushed the washed pots to her mother without a word about the sunken one, then dashed back up the steep stairs of the kitchen.

Leila was hanging clothes on the line to dry in the sun. It was a perfect day to wash and dry clothes, sunny and warm. Naji cautiously approached her sister, picked up a few pieces of clothing, and started to hang them on line.

"So, what is the secret?" Leila asked.

"Ssss, not so loud." Again, Naji put her index finger to her nose and tried to hush her sister's loud voice.

"Okay, okay. But what is it?" Leila whispered this time.

"I have discovered the truth about *looloo*!"

"Oh, yeah?"

"Yes," Naji whispered and turned her head around to see if anybody was listening.

"So, what is it?" Leila whispered.

"It doesn't exist! It's what grown-ups are using to scare kids."

"Really? What happened? How did you discover it?"

"I spoke with the *lahaf-dooz*. He sounded like a nice grandfather. He has many children and grandchildren. One of them is my age, and her name is Miriam. She is a human, just like you and me," Naji explained.

"Oh, she is a human?" Leila asked.

"That's right. And so, then, is the *lahaf-dooz*. I also remember that every time we have the pool man here to drain and clean the pool, he looks and acts like a human too. So, these two are not *looloo* monsters. I figured it out—they all are humans."

"Oh, really?" Leila smiled. "Are you very sure, little sister?"

"Yes, and my next step was to see if the pool *looloo* lives under the water. God knows how many times Mother has warned us about it. I sunk the shiny pot to the bottom of the pool on purpose—to see the bottom of the pool better. And to spot the monster if he touched it," Naji said with the conviction of a scholar.

"So what happened?"

"Nobody took the pot. It is still lying down at the bottom."

"So, what about the kids who disappear when they go out on the alleys without their parents' permission? How about the kids who drown in the pools?"

"Kids drown because they fall in the pool and don't know how to swim. The children disappearing—well, they could get lost, or maybe they run away on purpose. Maybe somebody human, not *looloo*, kidnapped them. I don't believe in the monster *looloo* anymore."

Leila moved her face near Naji's face and looked her in the eye. "Well, since you are older, and so wise now, I will share a secret with you. You are correct, there is no monster *looloo*. Grownups do use it to put fear in children's minds. So kids don't go alone on streets, don't bend over the edge of the pool, or do other dangerous things. It is all for protection." Leila spoke like a parent.

"Wow! So, I am right," said Naji.

"But knowing this doesn't mean you can go on streets by yourself or get dangerously close to the edge of the pool. With knowledge comes responsibility," Leila preached.

"Oh, I feel so much lighter, like a weight has been lifted," cried Naji, smiling broadly. It seemed to her that the heavens opened up and this new and less scary world appeared. She turned around and looked at the beautiful blue sky, the budding peach and cherry trees, and the sprawling vine climbing on the wall. They all looked so lovely. Sparrows chirped happily in sync with the melodious call of the doves and the cawing of the crows. She no longer had to be scared, stressed, or worried about *looloo* catching her. She took a deep breath. The courtyard air smelled different now, like early summer jasmine.

"Did you hear me?" Leila waited for confirmation.

"All these years, our parents scared me with imaginary boogie men," Naji said.

"As I said, it was for your safety. We all went through the same stories. But did you hear me? You must be very careful, Naji."

"Yes, yes, I heard you," Naji replied. Leila's bossiness annoyed her, now that she knew the grownups' secret. She decided to change the subject. "It must be near noon. I smell rice cooking. Are the men going to take a lunch break away from the dig?"

Chapter 9

The intoxicating aroma of basmati rice perfumed the air. Near the kitchen area, in the yard, the smell of chopped onions frying soon took over. Pieces of lamb and spices would eventually join the onions in the frying pan.

The two sisters laughed together while hanging clothes on the line. Leila could be funny when she was not under pressure. She knew many jokes. Naji was a perfect person to tell jokes to because she laughed easily.

About fifteen minutes later, Father and brother Ali arrived with two large tin trays. Ali carried a big tray on his head. On the trays were the lunches from the café for the workers, just in case the main dish, lima bean rice, *baghali-polo,* that Mother had prepared was not enough. They put both trays down on the ground near where the workers were still digging.

Ali was a fit thirteen year old who liked sports in general and loved running. He wasn't any taller or shorter than any other boy his age. Naji smiled when she saw her brother and skipped over to his side.

"I have to tell you something," Naji whispered to him.

"Let's get this lunch thing taken care of. Then we can talk. I've got to take the plates to the workers now," Ali replied.

Naji went down the stairs into the kitchen. It was dark and the smell of food was overpowering. The rice sat steaming in a huge copper pot.

Seeing that her carriers had arrived, Mother dished up the rice mixed with lima beans, dill, and lamb onto two large platters for the men and onto a smaller platter for the women. She piled the rice dish high, then sprinkled the top of each pile with a little white rice covered with saffron. The rice dish, *baghali-polo* resembled a mountain peak covered with golden snow.

Naji and her siblings climbed up the kitchen stairs carrying trays of food. Halfway up the stairs, the sound of call to prayer, *Azan,* struck Naji's ears.

"Listen!" Naji exclaimed and stopped.

"Come on, move. It's just *Azan.* You hear this several times a day," ordered her brother.

But this day was different for Naji. The second mosque started *Azan* a few seconds later, and not too long after that, the third mosque started the call. All of them together created a beautiful echoing effect that Naji loved. She looked up to the sky, looked beyond the peach tree branches, past the soaring doves, and listened to the melodious voices dancing together. Each caller had a different tone and his own way of extending and embellishing the sound of the words, creating unique moments. For Naji, the fragrance of jasmine flowers, the beauty of peach tree leaves, the flight of birds, and the dancing melodies of call to prayer, *Azan*, above her head culminated in a heavenly moment.

"Naji, keep going, the food will get cold," Leila prodded.

Her sister's comment brought Naji back to earth. She didn't mind; sometimes her short moments of escape created the most delightful memories. She looked over the dig and saw the men were washing. "They have to do the prayers anyway," Naji answered.

"Set the food down on the white spread and cover it," her mother shouted.

Naji set the rice platter down on the cloth as her mother instructed. She turned her head and looked at the dig. The workers were still at the pool, washing their hands, faces, and feet for the noon prayers, according to Islamic law.

She felt another strange pull toward the dig. The timing was perfect. No one was guarding it.

"Naji, go get the yogurt salad, *must-o-kheiar*." Father's command reminded Naji of the task at hand.

Her desire was to stay and get closer to the dig, but she loved and respected her father greatly. She would never allow herself to get sassy with him. She rushed to the kitchen. Her mother was preparing the *must-o-kheiar*, adding chopped cucumbers to a large bowl of plain yogurt. All that remained was to add a bit of mint, salt, ice cubes, and a good stir. She volunteered for the stirring part and Mother agreed. After a few strong stirs, the yogurt salad was ready to be delivered to the hungry men.

Carrying the heavy bowl of yogurt salad while climbing up the steep kitchen steps was not easy. But she was determined to finish the job right, especially since the job was challenging for her. When she got up the stairs, she saw all the men, including her brother, lined up behind her father, facing southwest, praying toward Mecca, the direction where all Muslims face to pray.

The noon prayers took much longer than the morning ones, which Naji had slept through. They involved lots of rising and bending and kneeling. She would have time to carry out her plan at the hole. Except—where were the women? Not in line behind the men. Perhaps in Grandmother's room.

The dig site had been abandoned. She put the bowl of yogurt down next to the rest of the food trays and covered it with a piece of cloth so bugs and leaves didn't get into it. She took a glance at her father and all the men; they were still busy with prayers.

Once again, Naji approached the hole, ever so carefully and slowly. Cool air caressed her face as she passed by the pile of freshly dug earth. Its fragrance tickled the inside of her nose. The closer she got to the opening of the hole, the faster her heart beat.

She could see the opening of the hole, even from several meters away. Glancing back one more time, she knew her mother, sister, and grandmother were rushing to start their prayers in

Grandmother's room. Her father led the men, focused on reciting prayers, bowing from the hips with hands on his kneecaps. In contrast to all the activities going on around her, the hole looked very quiet and patient. Naji tiptoed toward the edge.

"*Sam'i Allah-o-liman-HAMIDAH.*" Her father's voice reciting the prayers rang out across the courtyard, but Naji's thoughts were on the hole, her eyes fixed on the opening.

"*ALLAH-O-AKBAR!*"

Her father's voice caught her attention this time. So much louder than usual during prayers. Raising voices during prayers was how parents warned children who were getting into trouble.

Naji stopped and turned her head back to see her father's face. His eyebrows were tight. Clearly, he was disturbed about something. Naji scanned the area to see what could be bothering him. Finding nothing wrong, she turned back toward the hole and continued her slow, calculated steps toward it.

Her attraction pulled her like a magnet. She moved closer. The force felt much stronger than before. A small bit of the inside of the hole showed now, dark, quiet, and cool. She stepped closer ...

"Naji!"

She turned her head, but not fast enough to avoid Mother's strong fingers from grabbing her left ear. "Ouch!" Naji cried. "You are hurting me!"

"How many times have we told you not to get too close to this hole? Your father almost broke his prayers because of you!" Mother twisted her ear harder.

"Ow! But Mother, I was careful. Ouch, it hurts! Please let me go, I won't do it again. I promise ..."

Naji's pleas didn't help. Her mother pulled her away from the hole by her ear, tilting her face half-upward. Out of the corner of her eye, Naji saw her brother and sister chuckling.

"*Khanoom*, send her to me," her father requested, still sitting on his knees on his prayer rug. Her father called Mother *khanoom*, "lady" to show his respect. Mother let Naji go.

"Come here, my dear Naji." Father's calm voice soothed her frantically beating heart. Naji still approached him slowly, not sure what to expect. The workers sat around the food, staring at her.

"Don't be afraid, my dear. Come here and sit on my lap," Father said, tapping his left thigh with his hand.

The workers stared at her. They were hungry, but were not going to start eating until Father sat on the ground by the white spread and invited them to begin. Naji scurried over to her father and sat on his lap. He caressed her hair and turned his head toward the workers.

"Please, go ahead. Start eating and I will join you shortly."

"But sir," said the foreman, "you are our boss and the elder. We will wait for you. It's our custom not to start before our elders."

"No, no, please go ahead. I insist. We need to get back to digging as soon as possible." Father gestured his hands politely toward the food.

"Okay, sir, since you insist, we will start," the foreman agreed and then invited his workers to join him.

Once satisfied that the workers were following his invitation, Father turned his head toward Naji, who was sitting on his lap. "My little daughter, you have been a very good girl today. You have been a big help to your mother and to me. I know you are curious about the hole, but you must not get to the edge of it by yourself. It is deep enough now that if you fall, you could break your bones or, God forbid, your neck. We don't want anything bad to happen to you. So don't go to the edge of the hole, okay?"

Naji could not let the matter rest. The hole was irresistible. She had to risk Father's disapproval. Although he could easily ban her from the courtyard completely for arguing with him, she pressed on. "But Father, I want to see what is in it! If I'm not allowed to go near it by myself, will you take me there?"

"My dear, there is nothing down there but dirt. It is just a hole, a big and deep hole."

"But I feel there is something there. What if a genie or some horrible creatures are living in there that could pull the workers down?"

"Oh," Father chuckled. "I see. My dear, there is nothing down there but dirt, and even if there were genies, what could you do against them?"

"Please, Father can you just take me there?"

"Very well, I will. But not now. I am hungry, and we are behind schedule. Perhaps later, in the afternoon."

Naji let her biggest and brightest smile cover her face. "Thank you, Father." She got off his lap, kissed his face, and ran to join the women.

Her heart swelled with the warmth of victory. She had her father's approval on getting close to the hole and his agreement to take her to the edge himself. Nobody would be able stop her plan now, not even Mother.

Mother had already carried a big tray of food to Grandmother's room. Naji and her sister spread a white cloth, *sofreh*, on the ground and set the plates and utensils.

Naji sat near the window. From there, she could see the workers, Father, and Ali. One of the workers took the responsibility of pounding the meat for the stew. To Naji, the most delicious part of the lamb stew, was the pounded meat. But it wasn't just meat. Also mixed in the bowl were tomato, potato, garbanzo beans, white beans, onions, and spices. Someone strong or with a lot of tenacity would usually take the masher and pound. The tender lamb would blend with the other cooked ingredients to create a delicious mash that is eaten with bread.

"Please go ahead and eat," offered the worker who finished pounding the meat. Each man grabbed a handful of fresh greens from a large bowl and a spoonful of pounded meat.

"Naji, eat! Your food will get cold." Mother's harsh command brought Naji back to the women's lunch spread.

"Mother, can I please have a little bit of stew?" Naji asked again.

"No, the stew is for the workers. Your father bought it just—"

The door to Grandmother's room opened and Ali appeared in the doorway, interrupting them.

"Mother! Father, asked me to fetch more yogurt drink, *doogh*. We are out of it and workers are thirsty."

"Ali, just mix some yogurt with water, add some salt and stir it up. You know how to make *doogh*." Mother always spoke with affection to Ali.

"Yes, Mother, I know it's real easy," answered Ali.

"Then go ahead and do it, my son."

"Right away." Ali acknowledged Mother and ran toward the kitchen. It wasn't more than two minutes before he returned. "We are out of water. Can I run to the water reservoir, *ahb-anbar*, and get some?"

"Yes, my dear, go ahead," answered his mother with a smile. She favored Ali, always a polite, pious, and devout son.

"Oh, can I go with him?" Naji asked.

"No, Naji," Ali snapped. "I am going to run two blocks and then rush down the thirty-five steps, fetch the water, climb back up the thirty-five steps, and run back with a bucket of water. A little girl like you can't keep up with me."

"But it is dark down there. I can hold the lantern for you. I can run fast, I promise," Naji said and jumped up to demonstrate how quick she could be.

"No! Naji sit. Ali, you go," Mother ordered, crushing Naji's hopes.

Ali had a good physique and loved to run. He took the water container and a lantern and dashed out the door.

"I wish we had our own water reservoir like grand-uncle Akbar," Naji complained.

"But our neighborhood water reservoir is majestic. It has a beautiful opening dome and a wind catcher to keep the water cool," Leila said.

Naji really wanted to experience going underground again. She had been to the reservoir a few months before with Father. He let her carry the lantern. She remembered how dark, cool, quiet, and creepy it was at the bottom of the thirty-five steps.

"I'm back," Ali announced from the doorway, not too long after he left. He immediately went down to the kitchen and made the yogurt drink, *doogh*.

Through the window, Naji watched the workers, the mattress fluffer, her father, and her brother eating together. But her focus was not the men. It was what calmly lay behind them, next to the pile of freshly dug brown dirt. Her gaze took her to a world of unanswerable questions.

What if the dark brown, wiggly earth worms were not just innocent individual worms struggling to survive? What if they were spies for the creature living deep underneath? If the small worms could live inside the dirt, a much bigger creature could live deep underground too. In that case, since the small worms move so violently when their world is disrupted, how would the bigger monster react when—"

"Naji!" Mother's shout took her out of her gazing. "You have hardly touched your food. Eat. It is getting cold."

"You are so fixated on that hole. It is just a hole," Leila added.

"I don't know," muttered Naji. "It's still calling me."

Chapter 10

After finishing her lunch, Naji offered to collect the dirty dishes and take them to the pool for washing. Her mother nodded in approval. Naji put the women's dirty dishes next to the pool's gutter, and then went to collect the men's dishes. While near them, she eavesdropped on the conversation between Ali and Father. Their faces seemed so serious.

"I heard that the Russians have invaded from the northeast and have occupied the province of Azarbaijan. There are rumors that they want to occupy the north part of our country," said Ali. "Can that really be true, Father?"

"Where did you hear that?" Father asked.

"I heard it at work at the grocery store. A customer said the British have landed in the south, and that the city of Khorram-shahr is under their occupation now."

Father drew his eyebrows together. "I don't know, son. These days, it is hard to believe everything you hear."

A few minutes of silence passed. Naji collected a small number of dishes so she would have an excuse to go back and listen for more. She knew Russia was a country north of Iran, but she wasn't sure where British people were from.

Ali took a bucket of freshly dug dirt and dumped it on the pile nearby. "So, do you think we are going to have a war? Are Allies going to occupy our country? And if they do, are we going to have more freedom?"

"Son, we'd better leave the politics to the politicians. I am sure God will protect us. But don't fool yourself, no occupation is good. No foreign government occupies a land for the good of the people of that land. They all have their own agendas and will try to enforce them. We should always remember that and pray to God. May God give us wisdom to make the right choices."

Naji could not understand what all that talk was about. The only thing she was interested in was the hole and digging. She had shown a lot of patience by not bothering Father about his promise. But a promise was a promise, and it was time for him to deliver. She carefully approached him, knowing he must be in a good state of mind. She was preparing the right words when ...

"Sir, Agha, I am done with the mattresses," the mattress fluffer, *lahaf-dooz*, shouted, interfering with what Naji was about to do.

"Is it all finished?" Father asked.

"Yes, sir. Is there anything else I can do for you today?"

"Well, let me check with my wife," Father answered as he turned his face to Naji and asked her to fetch her mother.

Disappointed by the interruption, Naji did as Father asked. Her curiosity toward the *lahaf-dooz* was still strong. She hurried toward the kitchen but kept turning her head to watch him. He sat on the ground, expertly packing his peculiar equipment. His work fascinated her.

"Hurry up, Naji," she scolded herself. "These delays are not good. Father will forget his promise, and I will never get to see the hole up close." Naji started running, then—

"Ahhhh!" she shrieked as she hit the ground.

"What happened?" Ali called out as he ran toward her. Father came quickly after him.

"I fell down. Ouch! It's bleeding," Naji whined.

"You should watch where you're going, my dear. With all the workers here, all the tools lying around, the piles of dirt, the hole and so much happening today, you need to be extra careful." Father lifted her off the ground and looked at her wound.

"So, it's just a scratch. Ali, take Naji inside. Tell Leila to clean the wound and put some Mercurochrome to disinfect it, and then cover the wound." Father gave orders like a commander during battle.

"What happened?" Mother cried, running from the kitchen door.

"Nothing, she just tripped. Everything is under control. The mattress fluffer is finished. Do you have anything else for him?" Father replied.

Naji winced as the burning sensation spread through her leg, but she enjoyed all the attention. Her brother took her to the main room, where Leila prepared to treat her with Mercurochrome, cotton, pieces of cloth, and scissors. The little Mercurochrome bottle was old-looking and dark, with a cork on top. Naji did not like Mercurochrome. It stung and was red like blood. But she knew very well that she had to have it.

"It's going to sting, but it will kill bacteria and prevent infection, so it's good," Leila explained as she applied Mercurochrome at the cut on Naji's knee.

"It burns!"

"Quiet, little sister. It's all done. Now, lie down and rest," said Leila.

"I hate Mercurochrome."

Naji lay down on the floor on the soft Persian carpet and wished the burning sensation would go away soon. "If Mercurochrome hurts me so much, it may come in handy when the giant worms come out of the hole and attack us. I should keep that bottle nearby. It may force them to go back."

Leila laughed and left the room.

Father stuck his head into the doorway about a half-hour later. "How is your leg?"

"Praise God, *Alhamd-o-lelah*, I am fine, Father. Are you going to take me to see it now?" Naji answered, using the opportunity of her injury to get his sympathy.

"To see what?"

Naji stood up and got ready to walk. "The hole, Father. Remember, you promised me that you would take me to the edge of the hole so I could see inside." Naji made her voice sound like a very small child's. Father must say yes. He must.

"Oh, I see, you don't forget anything, huh?"

"No, and you promised, Father," Naji said. Had he forgotten? Will she have to beg again?

Father paused, watching Naji's limping-but-determined walk toward the hole. He shook his head. "Fine, let's go."

A big smile spread across Naji's face. With her little left hand, she held Father's big hand and they walked toward the hole together. Naji limped a little bit, for effect, but her scrape had stopped hurting. As they crossed the yard, she looked at the corner where the *lahaf-dooz* had been sitting. He was gone. On the other side of the yard, she saw her brother working alongside two of the workers, moving the newly dug dirt.

"Where is the third worker? I don't see him anywhere?" Naji asked.

"He is digging inside the hole," answered Father.

"What is the contraption over the hole?" Naji asked.

"That is how they get the dirt out of the hole. The worker at the bottom fills the bucket and sends it up. Someone up on the ground level receives the bucket, empties it, and sends it back for a refill. The pulley makes it easier to pull the heavy bucket up."

"Can you take me to the edge now, so I can see inside?"

"The edge is unstable. But I will hold you and you can look down for a few seconds."

Father had finally given in! Perhaps he realized that resisting her was useless. Naji would not stop persisting until she had seen inside the hole.

Father held Naji firmly. As she extended her neck, half her body was in the air above the hole. She peered down inside. It was dark, but she could see the digger at the bottom. She felt a gentle draft of cool air caressing her face. The smell of newly turned dirt was familiar and eerie. "How much deeper is he going to dig?"

"He is about twelve meters; he will need to dig at least another three meters."

"Can I stay here until they are finished?"

"No, your mother and sister are about to start their afternoon naps. Go and join them. You have had a rather busy day so far."

"Will you be joining us?"

"No, your brother and I have to help finish this job."

"I can help too. Father, please, can I stay?" Naji pled.

"Naji, you have been a great help so far. But it's best if you rest and then bring us our afternoon tea. Now go ahead and take your nap with the women."

Naji went to the main room with reluctance. True, she enjoyed summer afternoon naps, but with all the happenings in the courtyard, it would be more exciting to stay up and watch. She took off her slippers and entered the main room. Nobody was supposed to walk on the Persian carpets with shoes or slippers on. A sheet had been spread for her over the thick carpet. Mother and Leila lay on the floor, each covered with a white sheet. Anticipating more excitement, she placed her pillow on the floor near the window. That way, if anything happened in the courtyard, she could easily hear and see it.

A pleasant summer breeze blew through the open windows. The mesmerizing dance of the sheer curtains put Naji fast asleep.

Chapter 11

"Mr. Ahmad! Mr. Ahmad!"

Loud voices brought Naji back from her nap on the carpet by the open window. For the first few moments, she couldn't tell if the voices belonged to her adventurous dream or to the real world. She raised up on her elbow so as to lift her head high enough to see out.

Her father, her brother, and two workers stood near the dig hole. The foreman was bent over the hole and shouting into it. Father's eyes were wide with concern. It appeared that he was discussing something important with the others. In such situations, Naji stayed clear of her parents. If she bothered them, there would be consequences.

She caught Ali's attention and gestured to him to come over. But he ignored her. She left her place by the window and sat on the edge of the stairs. She rubbed her temples to ease the slight headache her afternoon nap had caused.

The headache continued bothering her. She knew the best way to get rid of this kind of headache was to wash her face. On her way to the pool, she carefully observed her father's and her brother's faces. There were definite signs of worry.

Naji knelt on the edge of the pool, cupped her right hand, and splashed some water on her face. She lingered there, near the digging, with her ears tuned, but careful not to get in the way. What could be wrong there? Her father's facial muscles were tight, as if he was clenching his teeth. The foreman was playing with his beard. He also looked concerned. The moment her brother got some distance from her father, she got up from the pool and approached him.

"Brother, what is the problem?" she whispered.

"We lost a digger!"

"What do you mean? What happened? Is he dead?" Naji fired all these questions at her brother with her almond-shaped eyes wide open. All kinds of thoughts were rushing into her head.

"Hey, slow down, sister, we don't know. He is not answering any calls and he stopped sending dirt up," answered Ali, still watching the workers.

"How deep is the hole now?"

"It should be about fourteen meters by now."

Many nightmarish ideas rushed into Naji's head. Now, at the depth of fourteen meters, the mystery was unfolding. Why had no one listened to her?

"What are we supposed to do?" she asked.

"You are going back to the room. Father is sending another worker down to investigate."

"Can I stay and watch?" Naji begged.

"No, go to the room before Father gets upset."

"Oh please—"

"No! Go at once!" commanded her brother, exerting his thirteen-year-old authority.

Naji understood that her brother was stressed, so she did not argue any further. On her way to the room, she saw her sister and mother, up from their naps, walking toward the kitchen. She stopped her sister and told her what was going on. Leila listened patiently, and at the end of the story, she continued her stroll to the kitchen.

"Aren't you worried?" Naji asked Leila.

"No, I am sure Father will resolve it. This is a grown-up problem. I have to go to the kitchen and help mother before she becomes my problem," Leila replied and continued her walk to the kitchen.

Naji, amazed by her sister's indifference, shook her head and went back to the room. She sat by the window again and watched. The knot twisting inside her stomach was usually a telltale sign of troubles ahead. "It has begun," she whispered.

Naji's imagination went into overdrive. What could have happened to the worker? What if he was dead? Oh! That would be so horrible. And bad luck too. And if he was dead, what killed him? And if he was not dead, was he lying unconscious in the dark? But why would he be unconscious? Is it possible the danger down there can creep up to the surface? What if the second worker disappears too?

"Stop it, Naji," she scolded herself. "Don't have these bad thoughts. Don't jinx it."

She stayed pinned to the window, watching every move of the people in the yard. The foreman was having a serious conversation with the second worker. Perhaps wanting to send him down the hole too.

"Uh, I can't stand it. It is difficult to see exactly what is happening and nobody is telling me anything!" Naji exclaimed and turned her head away from the window. She saw her doll, lady Nargess, lying on the floor all alone. She decided to occupy herself with her doll, certain that if anything happened outside, she would hear it.

"Mr. Hussein! Mr. Hussein!"

More loud voices from the courtyard interrupted her play. Naji peaked from the corner of the window. Her father's face was tight. Her brother and the foreman were bending over the opening of the hole and shouting as loud as they could. Naji couldn't hold her curiosity any longer. She rushed outside and ran toward her brother.

"What is going on?"

"We lost contact with the second worker too. He is not responding, as if he is dead," said Ali.

"God have mercy on them. What is Father going to do now?"

"He is sending the third person down," replied her brother anxiously.

"The foreman?"

"Yes."

"Ali, go fetch some more rope!" her father ordered. Ali jumped and disappeared to fulfill his father's order. That was a good thing. She could stay and watch.

The foreman stared into the hole. His skin was pale and damp. Naji thought he looked scared. She didn't blame him. Who would want to go into a deep, dark hole when two other strong men were already missing in there?

The foreman wrapped some extra rope around his shoulder and carried a bag with a few other supplies inside. Father and Ali were about to let him down on the rope, when Mother rushed out.

"Wait! Wait!" she cried, running toward the men, panting and waving her arms in the air.

"Let him kiss the Holy *Qur'an* and go under it, so God will have mercy on him," Mother said while holding the Muslim's holy book in her hand.

The men all nodded and mumbled words of agreement.

"What is Mother thinking? This is for when people travel far away! This man is not traveling," Naji complained to her sister, who had joined the group.

"This is for anyone leaving for a journey. It's a gesture of respect and total submission to God's will. It's for protection, Naji," answered Leila.

Journey. The word echoed in Naji's mind. Did her mother know something that no one else knew? She shivered in anticipation.

Father held the holy book in the direction of the hole and the foreman kissed it. Then Father raised his hand with the book up, and the foreman walked underneath it, toward the hole. Everybody, including Naji, prayed for him. Finally, the foreman disappeared into the hole, packed with extra rope, tools, a lantern, and plenty of prayers to accompany him on his journey into the abyss.

Each minute felt like an hour. What would he see down there? What happened to the other two? Were they unconscious or dead? What if he did not come back up? These and many other questions like them were passing through Naji's mind as they waited to hear from the foreman.

Naji noticed the shadows were getting longer. She knew that meant the afternoon was rushing away and soon, darkness would set in. She shivered, even though it wasn't cold. She inched herself closer to her brother.

"Ali, it will be impossible to search for the missing people in the dark of the night," she whispered. "What will we do?"

Ali shrugged his shoulders and turned toward their father. "What do you think happened to the other two workers?"

"I don't know, son. Perhaps some fumes down there knocked them out."

"But Father, what if the third man does not come back up either?" asked Naji, impatient with how Ali always brushed her off.

Father did not answer. Perhaps he did not have an answer for it. Her question brought up the grim reality of a much bigger problem. Instead, he moved toward the opening of the hole and called down to the foreman.

"Mr. Jalal, Mr. Jalal. Any news?"

"Yes, yes, send more rope. I still have farther to go," the foreman replied in a faint voice.

"Thank God, *Alhamd-o-lelah*, he is still alive," cried Naji jubilantly.

"Naji, be quiet," Leila elbowed her. The tension was thick.

"Help me, Ali," Father asked while trying to loosen more rope and send the man deeper into the hole. A few minutes and a few yards of rope later, they noticed that the rope loosened. Surely he had reached the bottom.

Everyone stood silent, waiting for a call, a shake of the rope, or any signal whatsoever from the foreman. Minutes passed by and no sign came.

"Mr. Jalal! Mr. Jalal!" Father called the foreman. His voice trembled.

No response came back this time. He repeated his calls several times without any result.

"What is all this hubbub about?"

Naji did a double-take when she saw Grandmother out in the yard standing next to them. Grandmother's chador was wrapped around her waist covering the top half of her body. Because of her curvy spine, she had to extend her neck and almost look up to see straight.

"Grandma, you won't believe it," Naji replied. "We have not heard from the first worker for almost one hour now. Then the second one went to investigate, and he disappeared too. Father just sent the foreman down. We are hoping that he can find the other two workers," Naji continued in a loud, animated voice.

"God forgive us, *Astagh-forellah*," said Grandmother.

"Quiet, Naji. Father cannot hear the workers over your loud voice," Leila snapped.

Naji tugged on Grandmother's *chador* and signaled her to the side. They both went to the corner of the yard, away from the hole and the crowd.

"Yes, dear, what is it?" Grandmother asked.

"Grandma, I figured out that *looloo* is not real. It is made up. Did you know that?"

"Well—"

Although Grandmother tried to answer, Naji wasn't asking, she was actually telling her. So she interrupted. "Grownups make up stories about *looloo* to keep the kids safe from dangers. So, I don't think *looloo* ate the workers down there."

"Yes, I don't think—"

"Since this morning, as soon as I saw the hole, I had this strange feeling about what was underneath. As if, as if, it was talking to me. Do you think it is possible that genies live underground?" Naji asked.

Grandmother looked at Naji to see if this was really a question.

"Well, dear, genies don't live underground. They are like humans and live where we live, but we cannot see each other," Grandmother replied.

"Have you seen one yourself?"

"No, but Mr. Hassan swears that he saw one many years ago," Grandmother explained.

Naji, deep in thought, wandered back near the hole where the others were anxiously awaiting news from the workers. The scent of the damp, freshly dug dirt attracted Naji's attention. A peculiar smell was coming from the pile. She examined the dirt. Fresh, dark brown, and almost velvety. She touched it; the dirt felt cold and damp. She saw a few worms wiggling, trying to get somewhere safe.

Suddenly, Naji gasped and took a few steps back. Leila turned and looked at her, and with a head gesture, silently asked Naji if something were wrong. Naji covered her mouth with her hand, ran back to the main room, and hid behind the curtain where they stored the bedding. Leila followed her there.

"What is it Naji? You are acting like you just saw a genie." Leila asked that question with an interesting choice of words. Was she thinking along the same lines as Naji?

"I j-just had a horrible th-thought," Naji answered, quivering in the corner.

"A thought? Okay, so you are not hurt or anything, right?"

"Leila, what if, down deep in the bottom of the hole, lives a gigantic monster who is the mother of all these worms. What if this monster swallowed the workers and will come up to avenge her children?" Naji frantically explained.

"I don't think the mother worm is any bigger than these small worms in the dirt pile," Leila replied calmly. There was no sarcasm in her words. That encouraged Naji. Maybe her sister believed her, for once.

"Just think, we don't know much about these ugly creatures, what they eat, where they come from, why they live underground, and hundreds of other things we don't know. What if there is a giant worm deep underground that is producing these little worms, and the diggers dug right through her open mouth and fell inside," Naji continued.

"Oh, come on. Nobody has ever reported seeing such a giant creature. This is all your wild imagination," Leila answered.

"Well, do you know why the workers disappeared?"

"No, but that doesn't mean—"

"We have to warn our parents," said Naji cutting off her sister's words. She ran to the courtyard without waiting for Leila. She was in such a rush that she forgot to put her slippers on. The stones in the courtyard stung her bare feet.

"Father, Father, wait! Don't get too close to the hole!" She was shouting and running toward her father as fast as she could. Naji was about six meters away from him when unexpectedly, she felt she was running on air. Her brother, sensing danger by her speed toward the hole, had grabbed her by the waist and pulled her off the ground. Naji struggled to release herself.

"Let me go! There's a great danger! I have to warn Father!"

Chapter 12

Father was on his knees, right on the hole's rim, bent over with his head inside it. His right ear was pointing to the deep end of the hole. He extended his left hand behind him, signaling calm and quiet without moving or changing his position. "Mr. Jalal, Mr. Jalal, is that you?" Father called excitedly, then paused and signaled again for quiet. "Yes, yes! The voice is faint, but it's him. Pull up, pull up!"

Father gestured to Ali to join him. Ali let go of Naji, told her to stay put and quiet, and ran to help.

"Be careful, it can be a monster trying to come up and attack us! Consider yourself forewarned!" Naji couldn't help herself.

Leila, ignoring Naji's warning, ran to help pull the rope, but her brother noticed her presence and asked her to move back.

A few minutes later, up came the first worker.

"It is Mr. Ahmad!" Ali yelled. Everybody's faces lit up. "God is great, *Allah-o-akbar*," came out of everyone's mouth harmoniously, expressing surprise and gratitude.

"Praise God, you look fine. Where were you?" asked Father with a big smile on his face.

"I will tell you in a minute, but first let's get the others up right away. Oh, sir, do I have a story for you!"

Everybody worked together, including Leila and Naji, to pull the workers out one by one.

"It's Mr. Hussein!" Ali announced the second worker's appearance from the hole.

"Mr. Jalal, are you okay? Are you ready to come up?" Father shouted into the hole to the foreman.

"Yes, go ahead pull the rope," he answered.

As the foreman's head appeared, Mother called to Naji. She handed her a tray with some freshly brewed hot tea and a dish of sugar cubes. "Go ahead and offer it to the workers and your father."

Naji knew the routine. Excited about the recovery of the workers, she wanted to get back to them as fast as possible. She didn't want to miss anything. It was a balancing act for her to combine a fast walk and careful delivery of the tray with the hot tea in tea glasses, china saucers, the sugar cube dish, and teaspoons. She looked straight ahead, and focused on her job.

First, she took the tray to her father and then to each of the workers, starting with the foreman. Naji listened carefully to the conversation. Her eyes were meticulously examining the workers for any clues.

"Yes sir, when I got to the bottom of the hole, I carried on with enlarging the bottom, as I was carving the east wall. Suddenly my pickax went through the wall like a knife on soft butter. I dug more. A hole appeared. I continued to dig. Shortly after, I felt a breeze; it felt like a much bigger space than what I had dug. Since it was very dark, to see better, I held my lantern up. To my surprise, it was a tunnel," the first worker explained.

"When *I* got to the bottom," interrupted the second worker. "I felt the breeze too. My eyes were not used to the darkness. With one hand, I was holding the lantern, and with the other hand touching and feeling the tunnel's wall. I walked slowly forward to find the source of the breeze. After a few moments, unexpectedly, my hand felt an open space. I raised my lantern to size the hole and I saw a tunnel big enough for two people to go through."

"Now, take a sip of your tea, Mr. Hussein." Father interrupted the flow.

"No!" shouted both Naji and Ali together in unison. "Please continue," Ali asked.

"I started walking forward in the tunnel at a slightly faster pace. However, I was very careful and aware of the ground. I had to make sure I didn't fall into a ditch, and I hoped I could find Ahmad's body. The best way to walk when the darkness is deep and the ground unsure, you know, is ..." He took a few seconds to swallow a sip of hot tea. "... is to drag your feet bit by bit. This way you know if you are—"

"Okay, okay, Mr. Hussein, we all know that. Just move on with what happened down there in the tunnel!" Ali burst out, lifting his body on his knees from where he was sitting crisscross on the ground and waving his hand. The poor boy could not wait even one more second.

His father gave him the "look" and Ali backed down.

"Anyway, I started calling to him, 'Ahmad, Ahmad,' as loud as I could. It was very spooky. Not only was it pitch dark, but it was also cold and incredibly quiet. I couldn't even hear my own voice, as if the sound were getting sucked in by the darkness. Suddenly, I heard Ahmad's voice from deep in the tunnel, calling back, 'Here, here!' I squeezed my eyes and saw a faint light waving. I assumed that was Ahmad's lantern about twenty meters down the tunnel. I told myself, Ahmad couldn't dig this entire tunnel by himself. What is going on?"

"That was exactly my thought too," interrupted the foreman.

Hussein took another sip of his tea.

"You know, I never thought my absence was that long," said Ahmad, the first worker. "It seemed like time was frozen down there. I was surprised to see Mr. Hussein, but glad that he made it down there, to be my witness."

"Witness to what?" Ali asked with his eyes wide open.

"Yes, what happened down there?" Father asked.

"Well, I hurried toward Ahmad when I heard his voice," said Hussein, the second worker. But I was still wary of the ground beneath me, so I had to proceed very carefully. When I saw Ahmad, he was very excited and asked, 'Who is there? Mr.

Hussein? Is that you?' 'Yes,' I said. 'Come here, come here and look at this, you won't believe it,' Ahmad said to me. When I got to him, it felt strange, like I was no longer in a tunnel. It felt like a much bigger space. My eyes were getting used to seeing in the dark. The second lantern, Ahmad's lantern, helped me to see a lot better."

Ahmad jumped back into the conversation. "Yes, then I showed him the bazaar!"

"What?" Both Ali and Father exclaimed at the same time. Leila sat frozen in disbelief and Naji started biting her nails, which she had never done before.

"Yes, sir, swear to God, *be-Khoda*, there was a big open area with sections like stores, but the entrances to many of them were boarded up and closed. I could get into one or two of them, and each was full of wares, such as fabric, materials, and other things," yelled Ahmad with excitement.

"Well, what he showed me was like a bundle of fabric or something of that sort. But when I touched it, it turned to dust," Hussein said.

"And then I showed him the bazaar!" Ahmad stressed that point again.

"Yes, then Ahmad took me to several other spots like that," Hussein supported Ahmad's testimony. "It did ... it did look like it was a bazaar of some form," Hussein continued. Ahmad moved his head up and down vigorously and looked at everyone.

"Mr. Jalal, what do you think? Did you see the same things these two are proclaiming? Or do you think they inhaled some sort of fumes down there and it got to them," asked Father in disbelief.

"Well ...." The foreman started to say something, but then he paused and started scratching his beard. No, actually it was more like rubbing his beard while he was thinking. Then he nodded his head back and forth in approval.

"It was amazing. I went through the same experience as Hussein explained. It was pretty dark down there, even with three lanterns you couldn't see everything." He continued rubbing his beard. "The place seemed like a big opening with symmetric compartments. Ahmad and Hussein showed me things that looked like bundles of fabric and other materials, but when we tried to pick them up, they turned to dust. They must have been very old."

"As if it were magic," Ahmad jumped in the conversation again.

"Magic!" Naji shouted. "I knew there was something down there. Didn't I tell you all? I felt it, I was drawn to it. A city underneath a city, imagine that? And you all laughed at me!"

"Calm down, Naji!" Leila advised her sister.

"Did you bring any of the items with you?" Ali asked.

"How could we? Whenever we touched anything, it turned to dust," exclaimed Ahmad. "But if master permits, we can go down again and search for objects that we can actually bring up," Ahmad said, his eyes eager and focused on Father. The other two also nodded their heads in support of Ahmad's request.

Father shook his head and gave a little snicker. "No, gentlemen, I am thinking that the fumes down there made you all hallucinate a bit."

"No sir, we swear, what we told you is the truth," Hussein defended his claim.

"At this point, I don't care. We need to finish the job. Our only toilet is out of order and my family needs a working outhouse," Father replied.

"But Father—" Naji exclaimed.

Leila smacked Naji gently on the side. "Ssss, quiet! Don't interfere."

"Brother, will you talk to Father and change his mind?" Naji whispered in her brother's ear, trying to salvage the search.

"No, he's right. I don't want to get in trouble," her brother answered.

The diggers shook their heads in disbelief.

"Come on, *yal-lah*. It is getting dark. We have lost a lot of time. Let's finish the job," Father ordered.

With that comment, the workers quickly drank their tea, got up and went back to finish the outhouse.

Naji and Leila began picking up the tea glasses, saucers, and other items that did not belong to the digging. Naji stopped and stared at the dig.

"See," Leila advised, "there were no *looloo* monsters down there. And no genies either. You don't need to worry about monsters anymore."

Naji's gaze was a telltale sign of her imagination at work. She wasn't sure if she was relieved from the danger of monsters coming up or disappointed that she didn't get to explore the mysterious underground city.

"Yes, sister, but they found something better, a city underneath! Who lived there? What did they do? What color were those fabrics?"

Leila rolled her eyes and as she was picking up the dishes said, "We must honor Father's wish. Forget about it."

"Maybe one day, someone will re-discover it and then …." Naji stopped and looked at the dig one last time. "And maybe that someone will be me."

Glossary

Ahbghosht: Iranian lamb stew.

Ingredients are lamb, tomato, potato, garbanzo beans, white beans, onions, and spices. There are two parts to *Ahbghosht*: a broth and *gosht-koobideh*, which means pounded meat. *Ahbgusht* is easy travel food and shepherds would take it in a pot on the road and into the fields with them.

Agha: Sir or Mister.

Ahb-anbar: Drinking water reservoir.

Many decades ago, *ahb-anbar* was part of the Iranian water storage and distribution system. These were built below ground level. The water was supplied from a network of smaller underground canals or deep wells. Some of them are considered marvels of architectural and engineering design.

Allah: God.

An Arabic word. Predominantly used by Muslims.

Alborz: A large mountain range north of Tehran. *Damavand* peak, the fourth highest peak in the world, is located on the Alborz range.

Alhamd-o-lelah: Praise God.

This is an Arabic expression often used by Muslims.

Allah-o-akbar: God is great.

This is an Arabic expression often used by Muslims.

Ahl: A witch-like demon believed to hunt mothers with a newborn child.

Azan: Muslim's call to prayers.

It is to be recited before every daily prayer. In Muslim countries, this melodious reciting of Arabic verses is heard throughout the cities to announce the time for prayers. Before the invention of loud speakers, the person who calls Muslims to prayers would climb up the Minarets and recite the call for prayers as loud as he could. He had to be able to project his voice over vast distances and pronounce words correctly.

Azarbaijan: A region northwest of Iran.

From the north, this region borders Armenia and the Republic of Azerbaijan (formerly part of the USSR). From the west, it borders Turkey. Currently, this region is divided into four provinces in Iran. People who live in the Azarbaijan region speak Turkish.

Baghali-polo: An Iranian dish.

It is prepared with basmati rice, dill, and lima beans. This dish can be served with chicken, red meat (usually lamb) or plain yogurt.

Bread, Persian style: Bread is an important part of the Iranian diet. The four major bread categories are:

    Lavash - This bread is very thin, similar to a tortilla. It is made of flour and the dough is rolled out flat and slapped against the hot walls of an oven, *tanoor*. It comes in either a large square or a circle, two or three feet tall and about two feet wide. This bread is the most useful, because it can be stored for a long time. It dries quickly, but a little sprinkle of water brings it back to eatable form.

Sangãk – is triangular in shape. It is a flat bread about three feet long. *Sangãk* in Farsi, the official language of the Persian people, means "small pebble." This bread is traditionally baked on river stones and comes out of the oven with some pebbles stuck in it. So the buyers need to make sure to take all the pebbles out before taking the bread home. Historically, *Sangãk* bread was the bread of the Persian Army. Each soldier carried a small bag of pebbles, which were brought together at camp to form a "*Sangãk* oven" to cook bread for the entire army.

Barbary - This bread comes in a circle or long oval shape. It is puffy and thick, with a brighter yellow color than *Sangãk*. This bread was originally brought to Persia by a group of Mongols known as Barbars. They settled in Iran and northwestern Afghanistan.

Tahftoon - This is circle-shaped flat bread, about 16 inches in diameter.

Bazaar: Marketplace.

Usually comprised of several city blocks of shops.

Be-Khoda: An abbreviation of "I swear to God."

Chador: A cloth material the length of a woman's body, usually worn over the head to cover the woman from head to ankle.

The chador is an easy and popular way of quickly covering a woman's body. The material for chador comes in many different colors and patterns. However, solid black ones are more common, especially for formal occasions.

There are many different interpretations of what part of a woman's body should be covered. The two extremes of these opinions are conservative Muslim communities and liberal Muslim communities. In most conservative Muslim communities, women are totally covered, even their faces. Women cover their faces completely, leaving only small openings or a black net around their eyes so they can see. On the other side of the spectrum, in the liberal Muslim communities, women wear their regional clothing or dress like modest western women. Where Naji lived, women were supposed to cover their hair and body, but their faces, hands, and feet did not need to be covered.

Doogh: A popular yogurt-base drink. It is a mixture of plain yogurt with water and salt. Sometimes dried mint is added for extra flavor.

Faloodeh: A frozen dessert made of thin vermicelli noodles, corn starch, rose water, lime juice, and sometimes ground pistachios. It is a tasty summer treat in Iran.

Farsi: The official language of the Iranian people.

Hoze: A utility pool that was/is used for bathing, to wash dishes and clothing.

Iran: A country in Western Asia. (The region is usually referred to as the Middle East.)

Iran is home to one of the world's oldest continuous major civilizations, with settlements dating back to 7000 BC. The first Iranian dynasty formed during the Elamite kingdom in 2800 BC. Iran is the eighteenth largest country in the world. Iran's neighbors are the Republic of Azerbaijan and Armenia to the north-west; the Caspian Sea (the largest lake in the world) to the north; Turkmenistan to the north-east; Afghanistan and Pakistan to the east; Turkey and Iraq to the west; and finally the waters of the Persian Gulf and the Gulf of Oman to the south. The official language of Iran is Farsi (or sometimes called Persian.)

Islam: A religion based on the holy book known as the Qur'an and the teachings of the Prophet Muhammad.

Islam literally means submission to God. It is reported that about 23% of the world's population believes in Islam. There are two major sects: 87-90% are Sunni and 10-13% are Shiite.

Jaroo, or Jharoo: Broom. It is usually referred to as a grass broom.

In old Iran, brooms were usually made from *Jaroo* brushes. The ones used by most households were about three feet tall and shaped like a triangle with a handle at the end. The bottom part was neatly cut to create an even and wide end to cover a wider area for sweeping. The handle part was pressed and bound together with wires to form a small handle.

Genies: in Farsi they are called *Jenn*, a creature known by many as fictional and supernatural. However, Islamic theology teaches that *Jenns* are creatures made from "smokeless fire" by God, in the same way humans are made from earth. Many Muslims believe that *Jenns* live in a parallel world to mankind, and together with humans and angels make up the three sentient creations of God.

Khanoom: Lady; madam. A polite way to address a woman or a girl.

Khorramshahr: A port city in southwestern Iran.

Kaman: Bow.

Lahaf-dooz: Mattress fluffer, a street tradesman that fluffs the cotton in mattresses. They use a large wooden bow-like tool with a single string that connects the two sides of this tool. This part is called *Kaman*. He pounds a large hammer-shaped mallet, called *Tokhmagh*, onto the string over piles of cotton. The vibration of the string separates the cotton pieces from each other and fluffs them.

Lavash: See Bread, Persian style.

Looloo: Monsters.

Mercurochrome: The name Mercurochrome is commonly used for an over-the-counter antiseptic. It used to be applied to cuts, scratches, and sometimes burns. The actual substance is Merbromin, which is used as a topical antiseptic. Its color is dark red and stains the skin when it is applied.

Mosque: A place of worship for Muslims.
Mosques are the center for prayer, religious education, information, and dispute settlement.

Muslim prayers: Islam requires believers to pray five times a day. Mosques are the place Muslims can gather for prayers and worship. However, they don't have to go to a mosque for prayers. Before every prayer, Muslims are required to wash their hands, face, and feet.

Muslim: The followers of Islam are called Muslims. The literal meaning of Muslim is "one who surrenders" or "submits" to the will of God.

Must-o-kheiar: A yogurt salad. A traditional Iranian side dish that goes well with almost everything. It is made with creamy plain yogurt, diced cucumbers and mint. It is one of the most popular yogurt salads in Iran.

Nahmoos: virtue; honor.
In the Middle East and Muslim world, *nahmoos* is mostly related to the honor of protecting the

women of the family such as the daughter, wife, mother, sister, etc.

Namaky: A street vender who exchanges salt blocks for dry bread.

People exchanged their dry old bread for salt rocks. In the old days that was a way for people to get their salt without spending money.

Noon-e-Khoshck: Dried bread.

Persian carpets: Carpets and rugs that are designed and made in Iran.

In the old days, Persian carpets were made by hand. Persian carpet is an essential part of Persian art, culture, and life. The oldest Persian carpet found is dated to 500 BC. Often, Persian carpet is the only flooring used. Its soft, thick wool provides a comfortable surface for walking, sitting, and sleeping.

Qur'an: Islam's holy book.

The word Qur'an is also written as Quran or Koran. Muslims believe that the Qur'an is the final instructions and revelation of God to mankind. Muslims believe that the Qur'an was revealed to the prophet Muhammad by the angel Gabriel.

Salahm: Hello

Salahm Agha: Hello sir.

Samovar: A metal container or boiler that is used for heating water to prepare hot tea.

Samovars are typically crafted out of copper, brass, bronze, silver, gold, tin, or nickel. A traditional *samovar* consists of a large metal container with a faucet near the bottom and a metal pipe running vertically through the middle.

Sam'i Allah-o-liman-hamidah: A prayer used during Muslim daily prayers, it means God heard him who sent his praises to.

Sangãk: See Bread, Persian style

Sofreh: A spread similar to a table cloth, which is placed on the ground before every meal.

Food items, plates and other culinary items are put on this spread to keep them clean. People sit on the ground around the *sofreh* and eat.

Tahftoon: See Bread, Persian style

Tehran: The capital city of Iran.

Tehran is a large, modern metropolitan city now. Population of Tehran in 2012 was reported over 12 million. Tehran is also Iran's largest urban area and the 5th-largest city globally.

Yal-lah: A slang word with many meanings. In this story, it is used for hurry up.

Study projects

1.   Research Persian cuisine. Go to the library or online to find out about different Persian food: soups, stews, rice dishes, barbeques, etc. Select one dish from each category, print color photos, and write down the recipes of your choice.

2.   Write a short essay on how earthworms eat, breathe, and multiply. Do earthworms have mothers?

3.   Draw a picture of Naji's courtyard and house. What are the differences between Naji's house and houses in your neighborhood?

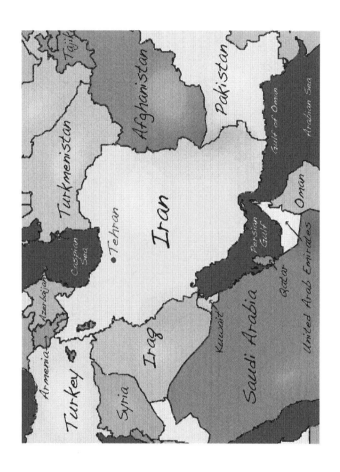

ABOUT THE MIDDLE EAST

1-   The Middle East is an important region in our world. Create a map of the Middle East region, include each country's name, capital city, and population.

2-   Research how many religions are in the Middle East. Create a chart that shows major religions of that area and their sub-divisions.

3-   Iran (also known as Persia) is a country with a long history. Create a time line of at least 15 notable moments in Iran's history beginning as far back as 3000 B.C.

4-   Go to the library or online to find recipes for Baghali-polo, Ahbghosht, and one other Persian food of your choice. Select the one you would like the most and with adult help, prepare this dish for friends or classmates.

5-   With the help of your classmates, create a class Middle Eastern Cuisines Cookbook. In addition to the recipes, each student should write one paragraph explaining the origin of the recipe they chose.

6-   Go to the library or online to find out what continent the country of Iran is located in. Who are her neighbors? How big is Iran? How many people live in Iran? What is Iran's main source of income?

7-   How important are prayers for Muslims? How often are they supposed to pray? What is the call for prayer called? Go online and record a sample of a call for prayer and play it for your classmates. Is it music?

DISCUSSION QUESTIONS

1-   Describe the main character, Naji. What was she afraid of? What did she learn?

2-   How was Naji's relationship with her parents? How was her relationship with her sister? How did she treat strangers? And why?

3-   Describe the other characters of the story such as the father, the sister, the mother, the brother.

4-   Was Naji's fear of the monsters real? Were the monsters real?

5-   How did Naji deal with her fear of monsters?

6-   What is the sixth sense? Did Naji have a strong sixth sense?

~ V ~

7-   Was Naji allowed to go on the street and play? Why?

8-   Do you think the diggers really found a city underneath the court yard? Explain why?

9-   What do you feel is the most important message of this story?

Explore more at

www.najistories.com

~ VI ~

About the Author

Vahid Imani was born and raised in Tehran, Iran, and made the United States his home in 1979. Coming from an old civilization, he is fascinated by ancient cultures and archeology. He earned a master's degree from Gonzaga University's School of Business, Spokane Washington, in 1980.

An enthusiast of fine art, he has been creating music, poetry and stories since he was seven years old. He is father of three children and grandfather of two (so far). Currently, when he is not dreaming about his next book, he is teaching music and classical guitar to children of all ages.

39195586R00123

Made in the USA
San Bernardino, CA
20 September 2016